The Man & The Moth

The Man & The Moth

Ethan Campbell

Pala Publishing
2015

First Printing: 2016

ISBN: 978-0-646-95317-5

Pala Publishing

Brisbane, QLD

palapublishing.wordpress.com

Cover Design by Chanae Jordaan

For Rebecca

Who always made time.

Acknowledgements

I would like to thank: My family, for their love and encouragement.

My friends, for the time, I will no doubt continue to waste.

Naomi, for her endless support.

Daisy the Dog, for her optimism.

Part I:

As the Angel Hung Suspended

You know you're living in a miserable place when it's a surprise that it isn't raining. The thought crossed Charles's mind as he dragged himself from the stained block of fibres that had once resembled a bed. A beam of unfiltered light caught his eye, alerting him to the open window. Jane sat at the ledge, her thin legs draped above twenty floors. Her hair blowing in the slight wind, almost blonde in the sun's heat. It was a familiar and welcomed sight. Charles would often find her lingering at the window, an optimistic oddity that always brought a smile to Charles's sunken demeanour. Such things made her feel alive, made her feel happy. Personally looking down upon the streets of Sector 23 made Charles feel naught but disgust; at the decay of both the buildings and the moral fibre of those who would begrudgingly call those streets home. They weren't all bad people. No one is born bad. They are simply the products of their environment and the environment of Sector 23 was but a hotbed of disease, violence and makeshift mob rule. The populaces had little access to morality; it was just the laws of Darwin, the law of *the Jungle*. Charles was not pious enough to pity them; he reserved only as much sympathy as he considered practical.

Jane turned to face him as he approached, knowing his gaze was fixated upon her.

"February 12th 2078, a dry London, we should mark it on the calendar."

He was halfway turned around when he realised the sarcastic tone she used, implying a joke. A few moments passed. Jane smiled, a smile of both embarrassment and subtle contempt. The way Jane smiled often haunted Charles. Her smile was more beautiful than that of a joyous blushing bride on her wedding day, yet in nature hollow.

"Are you working today?"

"Night shift, start at 8."

His words croaked out like a broken whisper.

Jane proposed a trip to Sector 12 for a glimpse of luxury, Charles nodded his sunken head in agreement, and not that he really had much choice in the matter. Jane got changed into a yellow summer dress adorned with red flowers, reflecting her auburn hair. The dress hugged her slim hips, and brought focus toward her blue eyes. In the years in which they had known each other, she had barely aged a day. Often they joked that Jane was the most beautiful women this side of the city walls, not that it was saying much. Jane's skin tag clearly visible across her right forearm, for a person with such aspirations of leaving this hellhole, she sure didn't mind showing off where she came from, where she had come from wasn't very nice. The day The Union took control Jane was assigned to Sector 24, she was set up in a corn syrup production facility. It was dark, noisy and most weeks ended with more than a few broken bones. After a month of begrudging labour, Jane staged what would have once been called a strike, it lasted less than a day and resulted death threats and a blacklisting from every Union facility in the Jungle. Seeing as The Union own every legal business and some others that aren't, this lead Jane into unemployment. Her art wasn't selling and she filled her time with altering her tired old clothing. Charles was always feigning his enthusiasm for her creations, though he did enjoy the sense of fulfilment it brought her.

Charles on this day, like every other day, opted for sleeves, the tag number embroidered upon the jacket. Charles hated displaying his tag, in his mind no one owned him, though the world he lived in and life he led all suggested the opposite. Below his human serial number, lied a microchip containing all the information of both a biography and full physical examination. You can't escape who you are anymore, and if you try you'll walk away without your arm and likely to lose much more.

Jane opened the door into the corridor leading to a broken lift. The fire escape always a difficult premise. Twenty floors of hard, too-short stairs covered in thick layers of grim, filth and over-touchy couples too engrossed in each other's company to notice their passing. The stairwell was much the same only the smell of the vomit, semen and other excrements wafted more freely. The fire escape was always the better option.

The streets were empty, except for the omnipresent waste left from the night before, reminding Charles that the world had in fact not ended. Most days Charles felt that he wouldn't really mind if it did. Passing through the Sector was sufficiently easy this early in the morning; half the population was in recovery from last night's exploits whilst the other half were probably still drunk. Sectors were essentially towns, living communities, factories and slums to house the workers. Sector 23 consisted of a series of energy based factories and a car production facility, besides that there is prostitutes, pimps and drug dealers.

They arrived at the over-rail in less than ten minutes. Jane and Charles sat in a solitary carriage, as the train carved across the landscape. In minutes they would be in Sector 12. Charles spent the bulk of the journey staring at Jane, something was different. He'd hoped to distinguish this before arriving in Sector 12 to show her his attention to her details. Though he was having no such luck.

Jane's gaze however remained fixated upon the view, despite the speed the scenery changed in a manner similar to the way in which grass grows. You don't notice it at first, you look away for a while and once your attention is returned the grass has grown an inch; they started their journey in a shithole, moments later they arrived in a slightly better shithole and soon arrived in sector 12, the greenest grass that Charles's pay grade allowed them to tread on. The door slid open revealing Sector 12, five by five city blocks of 'what could be if you worked hard enough'. Jane's affection ran deep, she wished with extreme totality to cross the walls into the city, which was a faraway dream, so she settled for Sector 12. Charles believed he saw it for what it was, a ploy. Sector 12 was the only Sector outside the city without a debt function, instead of factories the streets held boutique clothing stores and cafes. This place was a façade, an empty promise of a better future for those willing to work. But that was the thing, no one makes it, at least no one Charles would ever know.

Despite his contempt for the town, Charles still found himself immersed in these streets rather often, Jane loved it and he loved her. Working in a factory gutting fish all day robbed much of his sole, these deficits having an adverse effect on their relationship, each day he found himself with less and less to say and each night Charles found her more distant. When he did attempt to talk to her the words seemed to come out impeded, so he forgot about his tongue's existence and showed her that he cared, by taking her there when he could.

Soon Charles found himself sitting in a dark café, rich dark; the pseudo artistic by choice dark that makes people feel delusional about how sophisticated they are. 'Edgy art' depicting the 'common man' in their natural habitat of the wild Sectors 18 through to 30 adorned the walls. The walls themselves were painted in only 'sophisticated' dark gold's and browns. Resulting in a compilation of what Charles hypothesised was how a regal turd would look. On top of all this 'culture', Charles had just paid 23 credits for a muffin. He almost longed to be at work, waste deep in fish guts, though such nostalgia would soon pass.

The doors blasted open, revealing Sector 12, an oasis of beauty when compared to the decrepit streets of the Twenty-Third. The City Wall stood less than a few kilometres or a few more than a few, but still near. The Eleventh was so close Jane could almost touch it, taste it, feel it move and pulsate within her bones.

A svelte woman in an intricate coat walked past them towards the over-rail. She seemed eager to pass into the city and get home. To this woman Sector 12 would not be so amazing, Jane thought she recognised the woman from commercials advertising toothpaste. Such a woman probably looked down upon this place. Life in the city would be significantly better.

They walked out into the clean streets; something that Jane had forgotten was possible. The cobbles were all in order and each street lead to fabulous shops filled with extravagant silk dresses for every season. Oh, to live in the height of fashion, that was always her dream. 'Charles may believe that such pursuits are 'superficial', maybe he's right but what else is there to idolise other than beauty?' Jane commended herself on this thought, as she lead Charles to a new café called *Cellar Door*, Charles attempted to explain the reference to her, she didn't really care, it's not like one needs to know the background of something to appreciate the thing itself. Jane ordered a large tea. As she stared into the complex shades of the shadowy chai, she pondered the shadows of the world. That everything has a shadow. That we all do, that some people and objects are just more open with their darkness, or something along those lines. Jane knew life with Charles ensured security among other small comforts. Though Charles was not the man she had fallen in love with. He was a tired, unexciting, messy bore. Their relationship has suffered greatly because of him, some days she questioned whether they really loved each other. Jane always carful to never pursue this line of introspection too deeply, for fear of what she may conclude.

Jane sat in awe, admiring her decadent surroundings, Sector 12 was a utopia for hard workers. Charles seemed somewhat more engrossed in the act of playing with his food.

"Is your muffin no good?"

Charles's reply came out in a near silent monotone.

"Yeah, but maybe not 23 credits good. That's an hour and a half's wage!"

'Charles is so cheap!' the words rang out through her head, she remained silent. Increasingly she was becoming upset by his stingy attitudes, he would never spend money on anything. Even when in Sector 12 he would refuse to splurge. Jane missed her job, sick of waiting around for Charles. In honesty, Jane was bored, so bored that she yearned to prick her finger just to feel something. Though Charles did get her there, to his credit he was once a great man who she had loved dearly; though his debt life had sucked much of the happiness from his bones. A once promising young surgeon, now a factory worker, gutting fish ten hours a day. He looked like it too. Charles never dressed flash before *The Union*, but he knew how to present himself, black hair cut short and slicked back, always clean shaven and he always kept fit, never any hulking muscles but still fit. Now days Charles looked dishevelled with a mangled beard, scraggly long hair and the gaunt anatomy of an individual long under the lure of various dangerous narcotics, not that Charles ever touched such stuff; too dangerous for him.

Jane took her dirty mess of a boyfriend up the road to an exotic dress shop, specialising in various styles catalogued from the nuclear wasteland formerly known as Paris. It was tragic when *The Union* destroyed Paris, such beautiful fashion and art obliterated in an instant. Such a waste. If only they agreed to pay the debt. Thoughts of such a reality ran through Jane's mind. Seeing the Eiffel Tower, Notre Dame, exploring the art, music and film. These were all things she had always wanted to do and see, but never had the chance. She wondered if France still existed, whether British citizens would be allowed to travel to Paris. She figured such probabilities to be unlikely.

Awaking from her daydream, Jane found herself perusing one of only a few racks of dresses. All bright and stylish, if not a bit outdated. Charles was sitting in the corner. His eyes focussing upon the knots and frays in the carpet, the image reminded Jane of days before *The Union*, when Charles would spend hours in rare-book stores, slowly surveying the spines of old novels, his face lighting up every few minutes. In the end the collection was valued at over fifty-eight thousand pounds, each book was either burned or seized by *The Union*. Jane was allowed to keep her art and her clothes. She figured them to be a better investment

A blue silk dress caught her eye. The colour of far distant sea water.

"Please Charles!"

Charles smiled, conceding to Jane's wishes. He looked at her with something like adoration, at least he did still find her beautiful.

The woman behind the counter smiled as they made their purchase, her gaze lingered upon Charles for longer than Jane was comfortable with. Under the various layers of grim Charles was still a handsome man.

Leaving the store, they were caught up in a storm of people; men and woman crowding and racing toward the Sector 12 hotel. Jane took Charles's hand and pulled him through the troop of hushed yet frantic tones. They were half way through when they saw her; *The Angel.*

Charles once again found himself where he did not belong. This particular shop attributed its regal nature to its collection of various garments and antiquities ripped and catalogued from the backs of affluent woman as they were marched to the chambers never to return. The populous were told that *The Union* nuked those who refused to pay the debt, though the rare valuable items which those countries housed always turned up somewhere. The Union's attack was not nuclear it was chemical, nerve agents rained from the sky and those with enough access to ensure their survival were tracked down and marched to the chambers. Charles recalled memories of activists called *the Dissented Patriots,* whom leaked documents confirming such actions a few years back. However, a few days later the activists conveniently confessed to forging the documents themselves, the vague orangey hew of their skin suggested that some chemical incentive had been applied. Safe to say no one heard from them ever again.

"And now such relics lay in our midst."

The words were audible but for only Charles himself.

Jane begged him to buy her a blue dress; it was soft and highlighted some of her more captivating features, so without too much of a process, he gave in. The cashier was well versed in small talk, a pleasantry women of such stature really engaged in with the likes of the ragged couple. A sale is a sale.

Charles in his zeal thought exiting the store would bring the pleasant promise of a nap before work; such prospects were soon timely swallowed by a swarm of rushing citizens. Jane grabbed his hand, dragging him as she pushed through the stream of people which soon arrived at the Sector 12 Hotel; a safe haven for those passing between the worlds of the affluent and the indigent.

That's when he saw her dangling between the clear opaque blue sky and the dark orderly cobbles below. Seeing was not comprehension, a process which would take several moments. Dark hair flailed in the subtle wind, her skin looked as though it had once been soft and delicate though rigor mortis had turned such beauty into cold hard marble, cracked by sprawling burst capillaries around her neck. Thick rope suspended her from a street pole outside what had briefly been the beautiful Angel's hotel room.

The angelic girl would spend her final hours, adorned with jewellery and an elegant dress, to the world she may have seemed perfectly normal but on the inside things would be different. Charles had seen such tragedy before, a lethal cocktail of great courage and severe loneliness. Charles hoped that the plunge was enough to snap the girl's neck; the thought of her stiff body jerking in the wind was too much. Shudders ripped through his spine, ripples of the unpleasant thought. 'No one should die like that, no one should die alone.'

Charles suddenly tasted the salt of his tongue and awoke from his trance to find a few solitary tears gliding down his ghost struck face. Reality dawned upon him once more, brought back to the real world. The world of beautiful dead girls. Jane stood next to him, petrified, grasping his hand as if to let go would cause her to plummet to her death.

"Jane!"

No response.

"Jane look at me, please."

Jane's eyes remained fixated upon the girl, the colour drained from her face, like an infant's first glimpse of blood. Charles scooped her up, like a fireman picks up a child.

They made their way through the pulsating crowd of people, all flooding and scampering towards them, toward the hotel, to get a better view. Minutes later they were back on the rail, heading toward home, Jane's cold head rested on Charles's lap as he held her. Her hands stiff claws, clinging to the contours of his ribs.

When they arrived in the Twenty-Third, Charles carried Jane to the apartment building. The journey made significantly longer than the standard ten minutes. She remained entrapped in a catatonic state. The thought of climbing the stairs brought a quiver to his legs, even before the first floor. His muscles ached and began to lose feeling, only to have the numbness replaced by more pain. He lamented his former fitness, he was pathetically out of shape.

Charles laid her down on the bed and in a moment she came to. Her face showed a depth of pain in ways which words would find themselves lacking. She made one remark;

"She's prettier than me."

Then sleep took her.

Charles felt bile bubbling up his throat once he digested what she had said. He convinced himself that she did not mean anything by it; people say stupid things when they have been in shock. He had seen many people blurt out the strangest remarks in similar states. He hoped that this was the case, or maybe a misguided attempt at morbid humour. Charles forced the thoughts from his mind.

He sat by and watched her sleep. Once the colour had fully returned to her face. Charles left a glass of water on the bedside table, not that the hunk of mangled stained wood resembled anything close to a table. He scrambled a note exclaiming his deep affection for her, but he had to depart for work.

The rail arrived on time and Charles descended into the dark carriage as it pulled him toward Sector 17.

The Seventeenth was another slightly better shithole. It was little more than a river, trawlers, a few houses and the *Fish Factory*; a large square cube filled with conveyer belts of fish to be gutted and the discarded men whom carried out the dreary task. The smell was enough to make any human spill their guts in protest of its rotten potency, but they weren't really human anymore; just shades of their former selves, stripped of humanity replaced by barcoded conformity, now slaves of society.

Every monotonous second in that hellhole was the same

Grab, Cut, Scoop, Dump

Grab, Cut, Scoop, Dump

Grab, Cut, Scoop, Dump

Grab, Cut, Scoop, Dump

Grab, Cut, Scoop, Dump

The mundane nature of Charles's working life was less than fulfilling; it's safe to say this was not the life he had envisaged as a child, though doubts remain that anyone would. The others working at the factory were not far removed from the sad tragedies of Charles's story. These were people who had once been builders, teachers, electricians and businessmen, respected members of the community, soaked in the blood of fish.

Dwelling on the tragedy of today's cataclysm brought a precarious interlude to the usual banality. Something about the girl seemed familiar, what that was exactly or why would remain a mystery. Something about it left him feeling ill at ease. Not that dead bodies ever made Charles feel chipper. Heaven knows he had seen his fair share.

An alarm went off on the corroding monitor that hung from the roof, alerting Charles to his inefficiency and a pre-recorded video of *The Chairman* played informing Charles of "the vital role of efficiency in the debts levitation". The video played until he resumed his expected efficiency. All intelligent thought absented from Charles as he drifted into his usual trance state.

Grab, Cut, Scoop, Dump

Grab, Cut, Scoop, Dump

…

Jane chocked on the air as she awoke from her slumber. Alone. Her lungs cancerous, the dust and decay was getting to her. Pushing her arms out, an action driven by shocked clarity. She heard glass breaking on the floor as her brain scrambled to make sense of yesterday's events. The Angel was so beautiful, so lovely. The thoughts ran through her, why would she do it? If Jane could live her existence, then the angel should have been able to also.

She forced the thought to the back of her mind. She would not allow it to consume her. She needed to get things done. Jane began by taking a shower, the water was icy and bitter but it would suffice. The cold beads seeped down her body causing her skin to tighten and her hairs to rise. She let her hands linger over herself, she found great pleasure in the softness of her skin. She felt as a human once more.

Jane began to sweep the glass and other such scraps littering the floor, the steady actions repeated ad nauseam. It seemed as if each area she cleaned, she would come back to only to find more filth. Jane soon decided this task wasn't worth her very precious time. Instead she left her apartment and ventured next door.

Claire opened the door; her face burst into an expression of weary gratitude. Claire had given birth a few months earlier, her son, Simon was a healthy fat-boy. Charles had helped deliver the baby in the living room, the entire affair was quite disgusting, but Jane enjoyed helping Claire. She was always so appreciative and smiley. Simon was almost four months old, his cheeks permanently rosy. He got food and saliva on Jane's dresses but she didn't mind. Jane loved children, she longed for the day when she might have one of her own. Something inside her told her she would be a good mother, but not now. Not this side of the wall.

Jane heard Charles drift through the corridor, the scratching noises of his drained mind attempting to open their door. Soon after the shower began spitting; Charles would be in there for some time, attempting to scrub the smell off. He was never entirely successful, something always lingered.

Jane changed Simon's nappy, the smell made her gag but his innocent smiling face all chubby and red made it worth it. She laid Simon down next to his sleeping mother. Leaving the two to join her own sleeping hunk of organic mass. Charles was lying on the bed spread eagled, with his head stuck between the pillows. Jane sat down next to him and flicked on the tube. Images of violence and sex flashed across the screen, the TV Company knew what people liked south of the City. She switched to the news channel. She was always more inclined to keep up on current events. They ran a piece on how the debt was going. Things weren't sparkly glowy but everything was on track and one day life would be normal again and she would be a doctor's wife.

The news then cut to a clip of the *Chairman*, oh, what a fabulous man. His topaz coloured suit, the dark polished shoes and the air of intelligence and the charm of an older man. Oh, how she adored him, politicians came and went but this man was no politician. He was a leader of men and he wasn't going anywhere. The Chairman spoke in complex words and rhymes which Jane could seldom comprehend, comprehension none the less she still felt confident in her brave leader. It was predicted that things would be back to normal within the next eight years. Still a while away but the existence of such an estimate was hopeful.

Charles awoke as the sun was setting; his eyes were still red and glassy as he softly pressed his lips to Jane's cheek. Her lips were far too foreign a territory. She once again berated Charles with his own clothing, getting him out was always complicated but newly awoken Charles always seemed more open to suggestion.

They once again exited the solitude of their apartment, into the darkness, with its dirty streets and even dirtier people that littered the paths and walls. Those young skanks, with their dresses torn and shorter than any dress should be. How she despised them and those who associated with them. The walk was always short though they would always hurry at night. The rail arrived and the two crammed into the carriage, filled with lots of makeup stained bodies all pressed against them. She wanted to throttle those tiny sluts. Charles didn't seem to notice, zombies don't notice much really.

Stepping out into the Eighteenth, they headed towards the café it would not be their final destination. Though, Jane had learned the hard way to eat before consuming alcohol. Less than a year ago, during what was intended to be a community street party but ended up closer to a riot. Jane had been bored by the company. All of them brutish shades of uncivilised. Feeling ostracised, Jane found company in a bottle of scotch. She usually didn't drink brown alcohols but she also wasn't feeling overly picky. Charles found her in an empty lot a few blocks from their building. She had been passed out for some time and predators were lurking. Charles picked her up and began to carry her home. An anonymous figure stuck Charles firm in the leg with a beefy cricket bat. He fell hard on his back, protecting Jane from the harsh ground. The figure, now multiple figures scrambled around them, grabbing at Jane's arms and legs. Charles cried out. His screams thankfully heard. A man, whose name alluded Jane, stepped out from the crowd, producing a firearm from the folds of his pockets. The aggressors scrambled. The man helped Charles carry Jane to their apartment. The next morning Jane would learn that Charles had saved the man's life a year earlier, after the man collapsed in the street. It was a lovely reminder of the goodness that can exist in all. Two weeks later the man pulled the same gun on Charles on his way to work, He almost killed him for fifty credits. Since that day the couple travelled a few sectors before indulging in alcoholic interludes.

The bar was a few blocks from the diner, Jane had been their dozens of times but never really remembered the name of the place. It was a concrete box, dark and dingy but safe enough. Safety weighed higher than beauty in the Jungle. They sat in a dark corner. 'Why would I dress up if no one could see me?' she wondered. 'Not that anyone would with all these, orange stained, skin bags!'

The conversation didn't much intrigue her. She inquired into how his day was and received very little in return.

"Ok."

"Just ok, really?"

Her tone gave away a little resentment.

"Just ok."

She was about ready to toss her cocktail into his face, though she found her drink empty. At least it gave a reason to get up and leave, plus she'd need something stiff to deal with Charles. Jane approached the bar and found the promise of several drinks waiting for her. Many men paid for a few seconds of her company. Though only one that she wished to converse with. Oh! He was fantastic! Fabulous really, any number of positive adjectives.

His hair was clean and perfect, dark and slicked to the side, filling out an Umber double breasted jacket, his shoes dark, polished leather.

Two hours left. Charles was beginning to tire. His back muscles tightening, the blood in his feet pulsating. A few more years working like this and he would develop a permanent hunch. Each fish was more tiresome than the last. A glance at his monitor revealed that he was operating at the lowest possible efficiency. It was typical this late in a shift. His ten minute break was scheduled twenty seconds ago, though seven more fish had to be prepped.

Stepping aside into what was called a break area but was actually a dark room with a few milk cartons littering the ground. The only light coming from a coin operated kiosk. Charles purchased a one hour energy shot, then sat on the damp floor. Other workers were smoking, all of them ignoring one another. Charles had once had a few friends at the factory though over the years, they had been fired, moved, others simply passed away. Alone it had become easier to slump into the darkness. Often Charles questioned his decisions in life. All the wonderful and tremulous seconds, minutes and hours of life which lead him to this dark grimy room.

A buzzer went off, coming from a speaker digging out of the ceiling. A robotic voice spoke the names of the men going back on duty. Charles was the last. He injected the energy shot, throwing the dirty needle into a pile of various trash lingering in the corner of the room. Once such an act would nag at his senses of morality, leave a twinge in his stomach. His sense of morality wasn't dead but it was on its way. He didn't look back as he made his way back to the work station. His knife resting on an unmoving conveyer belt. Every now and then, a human supervisor would stop by. Attempt to intimidate the workers into efficiency. Fire a few people just to make a point. On each of these occasions, it took all the will Charles had left within him, to not plunge his bloody blade into the carotid artery of any or each of them. When Charles closed his eyes he saw these supervisors flailing in the pools of fish guts, their blood fading into the pools of fish guts, slowly sinking, swallowed by the filth. This fantasy helped him get through the final hours of his shift. A siren buzzed, the monitor next to him played a video of The Chairmen.

"Thank you for your service. Thank you, for helping build a better Britain."

The alliteration would be stuck in his head the entire trip home. It always was. Likewise, Charles rarely remembered exactly how he arrived back home. A mix of physical exhaustion and chemical exhaustion insured Charles's dazed stasis.

The light burned as Charles opened his eyes. 'Maybe this sunshine crap was overrated'. Jane assured him the light would fade soon, right before barraging him with his personal effects.

"We're going out."

"Ok."

She managed to look dissatisfied at getting exactly what she wanted. Charles pulled on his trousers grabbing the first shirt he could find, dark and mangled with long sleeves; it would serve its purpose.

Jane and Charles once again descended down the fire escape. The darkness sheathed the dirt but it was still there, nothing would ever change that. There is and always will be dirt, scum, filth and decay everywhere that Man treads. In the Jungle they just couldn't hide it, just pretend it doesn't bother them so much.

Before they knew it they were in Sector 18, the diner was small and cramped but the food was acceptable and the lights were dull enough to allow for the occasional wink of sleep. Neither Jane nor Charles talked much. Perhaps they were too engrossed in their food, though it was more likely that neither had much to say to the other. Charles ate a greasy sandwich with enough mayonnaise to drown himself.

Walking through the doors of The Great Bloody Bear. The place was a dark miserable hole, but animals such as themselves use holes for nourishment and protection. A safe place to drown your sorrows, as long as you're on the inside. Outside it's the same mess of pimps and *wannabe* gangsters. So naturally, they try to stay inside.

Forty people littered the dimly lit room, the dull conversation and duller music barely audible. The décor reminded Charles of the shoddier sections of the antique stores he had frequented in his youth. Chipped foggy glasses, and scratched stained tables, with torn damp stools. The couple sat down at a booth in the corner.

The hours passed and Charles was drinking some form of brown alcohol. He just wanted to roll his eyes back and fade to sleep. Only Jane's barrage of questions ensured his consciousness.

"How was your day?"

"Fine."

"Really, just fine?"

"What else is there to be said about fish guts?"

His answer appeared insufficient. Jane stormed off towards the bar. Charles raised his arms in protest and tried to say "come back", but it came out closer to gibberish and his rigid arms flailing in the air looked pathetic. So he sat down once more with his face in his hands, sulking.

Jane's protest was more definite, his eyes found her standing at the bar, advertising the swing of her hips as she flirted her way through three drinks. She didn't let any of them get close, just enjoyed the view. Or so he thought.

After five or so minutes of sulking Charles looked up once more to find her laughing and smiling toward a man who to say *stood out* would be an understatement. He did not strike Charles as a man with features sculpted by god himself, yet one would objectively label this man as conventionally attractive. The man was average height, average build, and clean cut with slicked brown hair. He was wearing a regal turd coloured smoking jacket with a black satin bow tie. Such "class" was a rarity beyond Sector 11, an enigma that such a man would venture so far into the wild.

Embarrassed, tired and hurt Charles sank his head into his hands until whatever pride he held dissipated. Squeezing his fists till the colour ran from his knuckles. Despite his resonance he lifted his eyes to find an empty bar. Schism of nausea ripped through his gut. His legs ached as he sprang to his feet. The panic only multiplied as he approached the barman, who was less than helpful, just shrugged and continued wiping the bar with a rag so dirty that it was probably making it worse.

The fire of his churning gut did not ease as he made his way outside, the alley was empty and the street desolate. The bile spilled its way through him as Charles came to the realisation that Jane had left him.

The journey back to Sector 23, passed in a blur of solemn panic. Once he arrived home, Charles sat in the corridor of his apartment building by the phone in the hall, waiting for a call, an apology, a plea for help or even a goodbye. No such correspondence came through. Maybe this was her way out, the future she wanted that he could never give. Charles lay there on the dirty ground with only his self-pity to keep him warm.

"May I buy you another drink?"

He spoke with a vague accent that she couldn't quite place. They had been talking for a few minutes, light conversation. She was finishing the martini he had bought for her.

"I'll take a glass a champagne."

A smile flashed across his face as he spoke coy and confident.

"That region doesn't exist anymore, but sure."

Jane smiled broadly and stared at him with intent, hoping that Charles was witnessing the whole thing. She pictured his crinkled, jealous face only adding more legitimacy to the joy she was conveying. The Charming Man then invited Jane out into the alley for fresh air. He said Jane took the breath out of him. She was about to decline, though a glance back at Charles found him unmoved, still staring at the ground. He wasn't jealous, he didn't even care.

Filled with betrayal, Jane followed The Charming Man out into the cool night air. They stood in the light of the night sky as he smoked fragrant cigarettes and asked Jane questions about her life. Where she was from, what she does with her time. Finally she had a question of her own.

"Why are you here?"

He seemed both amused and impressed by the young woman's query.

"I work on behalf of Epsilon Incorporated, I oversee our community outreach program and I'm heading back to the inner city tomorrow."

"How interesting!"

She tried to keep the excitement out of her voice but found her speech a giddy mess. She was about to ask a follow up question, when suddenly cut off by two hooded figures, approaching rapidly through the darkness. The larger of the two figures, a bald headed flabby block, spoke first. His words a string of guttery vulgarity.

"Nice girlie *yous* got yourself '*ere*."

A cold shiver of uncertainty passed through Jane as the second figure, a tall, thin pencil necked junkie produced a blade from the pockets of his ragged coat. The rusted silver of the blade caught the moonlight as if to seal the Man and Jane's fate.

The figures approached with leering intent, her heart was beating so fast it felt like it had left her chest. The Charming Man however was calm and collected, he maintained the same casual upright posture that he had held throughout the encounter. His calmness confused and worried the girl, yet the bravado connoted a strange sense of safety.

The figures were less than a few feet away when finally the cool, collected man next to the frightened girl showed further signs of life. With a soft yet confident tone, he asked Jane to close her eyes, unsure of what was about to occur she decided to trust him.

For the longest second of Jane's life there was quiet. Nothing. Then the sound of the blade slicing through the air. Quite. Now the slicing again. Howling screams overtook the quiet and the frightened girl opened her eyes to find the larger man toppled over his partner, gushing blood and cursing profusely. The Charming Man chucked the knife into the gutter, it made that distinctive twang of metal on concrete that you always hear in the old movies. His soft, sturdy manicured hands met with the girl's delicate wrist gripping her as they ran toward the street. Adrenaline rushed, she could feel it passing through her limbs; she felt good, she felt alive.

A black car pulled up at the curve, she followed The Charming Man through the already open back passenger door without any hesitation; Charlie would have to find his own way home.

The inside of the car was just as beautiful and luxuries as it was on the outside, leather upholstery and tinted windows. The girl had never seen such a vehicle before; another of the night's oddities. The driver pulled out from the curb and made a hasty departure from the Sector. Quite the spectacle.

The Charming Man spoke with a tenderness and clarity that Jane had seldom encountered in her life.

"I'm sorry I ruined your night, we will get a hotel. I can take you home tomorrow, tonight it's too dangerous."

She noticed the faintest ghost of an unknown accent lingering in his voice. She stared at him confused,

"What danger? Those guys aren't coming back."

"Maybe not, but whoever they work for is sure to send someone else, the more work we do the less business goes to organised crime."

The car pushed on through the sectors, the curtains of darkness illuminated by the headlights. The roads between sectors run parallel to the rail. An outpost stationed between each sector, to check official documentation. This was standard procedure yet their journey went by unimpeded, greeted at each outpost by open gates. The driver made a joke about phoning ahead.

Jane was halfway through the comprehension of the statement when Sector 12 came into view. For the first time she saw the place at night. Looking out of the car window everything seemed distorted and odd. She realised that this place was a dark shadow of the true city. The real city never sleeps, there is never dark. Always illumination. Oh, how she longed for its warm embrace. Oh, how she hated life in the jungle, as if you could even call it life.

The driver parked the car. The Charming Man got out first. She watched him as he re-buttoned his jacket and walked around the car to her door, opening it and once again taking her hand. They walked through the darkness toward the Sector 12 Hotel. A few days ago the proposition of sleeping in this hotel would have brought her immeasurable joy, tonight however she would rather sleep on the cold, dirty street. Though in the company of The Charming Man, the street didn't seem so bad. She looked up at the streetlights, half expecting to see the beautiful sad angel drifting in the stillness but there was only the darkness.

The Charming Man took her by the arm and led her into the foyer, half a dozen men, mostly bald, built and packing large firearms greeted them. Jane almost screamed with despair. All of this just to die here, she thought as she closed her eyes, expecting whatever horrors that were to come. Jane's resolve was calmed somewhat when The Charming Man informed her that these new companions were under his employ. What seemed to be the leader of the bunch, a strikingly tall man with near white blond hair and the muscle tone of a Greek God handed The Charming Man the room key. Once again taking Jane's hand, The Charming Man led her up the staircase. The stairs themselves were intentionally unorderly and loose as if to instil the feel of an old, regal structure, the stairs also covered by a red carpet that was meant to look like satin but was really some form of polyester. This place on the inside seemed almost a parody of taste.

When Jane arrived at the top floor she felt her heart sink, only two rooms, one on the right, and another on the left. If they were to go left they would arrive in the room that the angel had once dwelled. They went left.

Arriving at the room, the honeymoon suite. The Charming Man apologised saying that this would be the only room which the thugs would not think to check. As she entered the room she gazed upon the shag rug, the wilted flowers by the bed and the impressive view of the Outer City Wall; she was filled with despair.

He held her close. She snivelled all over his jacket. He continued to hold her. So she held him tighter.

"It's okay, we've had a rough night."

He took off his jacket and placed it across her long pale legs, and for the briefest moment she fell to sleep. However a knock on the door once again sent Jane's heart racing. She screamed only nothing came out but tears. She gripped his arm tightly, she felt her nails dig into his flesh, he just pulled her closer.

"It's only room service."

The Charming Man comes back to the bed holding a bottle of clear alcohol. Neither of them bother with a glass, neither drinking for the taste. Jane doesn't read the label but she thought it tasted like vodka. Then it tasted like burning, she swallowed as much as she could. It didn't take long for the alcohol to take affect and once it did the world was cheery once more. Jane danced, sang and drank as her troubles seeped away. The worries flew out the window into the night air.

Before too soon her legs hurt, the world deciding to tilt a bit too harshly. So she fell back into the comfort of the large bed, the world still spinning, she moaned in the agony of euphoria and vertigo. His arms wrapped around her, catching her as she almost fell from the bed. In that moment the world stopped rotating. What happened next was a drunken haze of ecstasy and experiment, of sweat and saliva, of love and lust.

-RIIING-

-RIIIIIIIING-

The phone buzzed painfully and unexpectedly, Charles didn't recall falling asleep but here he was, wide eyed and awoken, in pool of his own drool.

-RIIIIING-

His hand slapped down on the receiver.

"Hello?"

It came out as a sort of cautious question

"Hello Mr Ryan."

The man spoke in a very posh manner which Charles had seldom come across, yet his accent seemed strange and even further out of place.

"Mr Ryan, I have something of yours."

He corrected himself.

"Someone of yours."

The ambiguity got in the way of the true message.

"A hundred thousand credits or the girl dies, you have twelve hours."

"Don't you, touch her!"

The words rolled out like a hiss carried through the winds of a silent night. The phone guest laughed in the sick manner of a man departed from the realm of earthly conduct. He was about to hang up when Charles asked,

"Where am I supposed to find that kind of money?"

The man laughed once more;

"That's not my problem, but if it was, I'd start at the late night store in Sector 15."

"I don't have clearance out that far!"

Charles lied, not entirely sure why, but he knew, the man just continued laughing until finally he hung up. Leaving Charles to resume his surging panic, the likes of which he had never conceived possible. Panic attacks is what they call it, objectively it's a treatable condition, manageable with therapy and medication. Yet right in that moment in the frightening beginning and end of the controlled chaotic existence that is his life. There was no measure.

Charles picked himself off the floor after what had seemed an eternity in seconds. Drool and sweat stained his jacket, that black mess of vinyl and leather. People more often than not believed he chose to be that way, but he was; what the world had made him. A standby mode fuelled by self-loathing. Jane didn't deserve that, she deserved to be happy, in whatever life she chose.

Charles pushed these thoughts out of his mind as he opened his neighbour's door with a spare key. Simon and his mother were out, she had to take him with her to work most days. All the other woman would crowd around him and squeeze his fat cheeks. The centre of attention.

Their twenty square metre apartment lay vacant, sprawled with the rubbish and treasures of their existence. Charles was only looking for one item, Simon Senior's *Colt Buffalo,* a 0.50 calibre revolver likely to leave any man unrecognisable. Charles always thought the elder Simon was paranoid when he said "they" were "coming for him". Simon proved Charles wrong when Simon's rigid corpse, void of eyes turned up on the streets. Notice the use of the plural. Streets.

The cannon was heavy in his hand, though the thoughts contemplating the nature and possible use of the weapon, weighed heavier still. A necessary risk.

The Rail journey and the walk that followed wasn't far in a geographical sense, yet the trip felt an eternity. Charles figured the caller would in all likelihood be the man from the bar.

The twenty four hour store was situated on one of the nicer blocks of Sector Fifteen. For hours Charles waited and watched the building. "Hard men" came through the premise and left without any apparent purchases, but money exchanged hands. Stacks and stacks of credits handed over. It took Charles a few minutes to work out that the place was a drop off for some form of organised crime. Now more than ever he figured the gun to be a good idea, or as good an idea as one can have when planning on robbing a store with gang connections in order to pay off a homicidal freak with great hair.

This further explained largely why The Caller would think that this was a good place to start. So Charles walked the strip for a little longer. Killing time, it would seem. At 2:00 am he saw his window of opportunity. The Clerk was in the back and no one else was in the store.

-DIN UHHH!-

"Shit."

Charles was caught off guard by the idiotic welcome noise. The clerk came out faster than expected, surprised and without caution; Charles drew the gun. Just not fast enough, a powerful arm grabbed at his wrist pulling him over the counter. Landing painfully on his hip, powerful blows coming down upon him. Things cracked and snapped, blood flooded Charles's nasal passages, and began seeping through his skin. With the last of his strength Charles reached for the gun and raised it to the man's chest. He had hoped the man would back off, but this time the man grabbed at the gun.

The shot rang out and the weight of the clerk collapsed upon Charles. Barely able to see, soaked in his own blood, and the blood of his victim, it being hard to differentiate between. Charles dragged himself to the cash box. Every second of it agony, white noise screams rushing through his ears. Seventy-two credits...

"FUCK!"

He screamed, falling to his knees, consumed by rage, he struck out at the man he had killed, his skin still warm. He repulsed himself, he had killed a young man in the peak of his life.

Charles sat beside the corpse. Weeping and cursing at the world. It took him almost ten minutes to remember that there was a backroom to this place. Dragging himself there, he found the safe. More white noise ripped through him. A four digit combination lock.

1-1-1-1

Not that simple, criminals are sometimes smarter than they look.

-BRIIIING-

The phone rang somewhere to his left. The noise caused spams of pain, in every known part of him. Cautiously he pulled the receiver to his ear;

"Hello?"

The replying voice was business like in nature and different from the first caller, yet distinctly eastern European

"9-4-3-3"

The ringer went silent. Dazed and confused, Charles entered the magic numbers and voila; a large stack of cash. Lying in a small pool of his own blood. He counted it. Seventy eight thousand credits. It would have to be enough.

More white noise. But it was never white noise. High pitched screams. Pulling himself up, he walked back into the store. That's where he found her. Found her screaming;

"Daddy!"

Huddled over the unrecognisable remains of what was once her father.

Jane awoke, bathed in rays of light. The sun shone even more brightly for today was the first day of her new existence. To her surprise, her head was not the least bit foggy. How humorous, the best sleep of her life so far, in the same building that, an angel decided to kill herself.

Again to her surprise, and pronounced delight, she found him asleep beside her. Only then did she realise that she was no longer in her previous night's dress. Instead a silk bathrobe. Embarrassment ran through her as she had no recollection of redressing.

As if sensing her shame, he awoke with his perfect blue eyes fixated upon her.

"I hope you don't mind."

He spoke as if he were the one at fault

"Not at all."

The Charming Man then kissed her softly on the forehead as his fingers combed through her hair. Today would be the first day of Jane's new life, and the hours were passing faster and faster. Abnormally so but that's what happiness does.

They didn't leave the room for hours. The outside world didn't exist, they showered together, ate breakfast and lunch in the bed. All the while conversing and getting to know one another. She told him that she was an artist, he spoke to her of artists he knew in the city. They talked of life beyond the wall. He was more than just a pretty face. He told Jane of museums and plays and galleries. It all sounded so blissful. So amazing. The hours melted away. As they laughed and embraced.

Only a sudden unexpected knock at the door broke Jane from her trance.

It was another of His men, an Arian colossus. Holding two black duffel bags. The first bag was handed to The Charming Man. The second, dropped at Jane's feet. The Charming Man took his bag to the bathroom as Jane looked through the contents of her own. Beautiful dresses in every colour, shade, style and fabric. One more conservative blue one caught her eye.

"Wear the short green one."

Short green one it was. The material, a mix of satin and cotton. As The Charming Man re-entered the room, Jane noticed that it matched

"What are these for?"

"Your new life."

Jane's heart began to race, as she ran towards him, they enfolded their arms around one another. So filled with joy. She had hoped that he would take her to the city but when her dream eventuated she couldn't contain her gratitude.

"We'll be stopping by yours to collect whatever belongings you deem worth keeping."

The thought of her final interaction with Charlie brought nausea and guilt, what is there to say other than goodbye? In honesty they had said goodbye a long time ago. Even though they had drifted apart it would be odd knowing that she would never see him or The Jungle again.

The Charming Man took Jane's hand and walked her to the car. The journey back seemed to pass in an instant. As if Jane's dread was pulling them towards the encounter. A blink and they were once again in the desolation that she had previously called home. The driver pulled up to the curb. Jane made a point of opening the door herself. The Charming Man busy starring at the limited horizons of the poor. Jane savoured every uneven step, every twinge and ache in her legs. Knowing that soon she would never know these imperfections again.

Jane's apartment, if you could call it an apartment was more or most certainly less than a complete dump; though today the description seemed far more literal. Tiny pieces of reflective surface littered the floor. The bed overturned. Dried blood stuck to the floor and door knobs. Charlie was nowhere to be seen. Jane left most of her belongings behind, all she took was a leather bound sketchbook. Feeling both relieved and worried Jane headed next door.

The key nowhere to be found she had to knock. Claire opened the door, the chain in place. Realising it was Jane she opened up. Inviting her in, they conversed for some time, she told Jane that Charles arrived home early in the morning, drunk and visibly distraught, that men in uniform had taken him. The baby Simon clung to his mother, Jane's fingers reached out and touched his cheek and the child burst into tears. Claire held the boy closer and he was again comfortable.

Jane told Claire about the events that had transpired in the past few days, it helped put things in perspective and the longing look on her face brought Jane some satisfaction. She told Claire that she could take anything of Jane's from the apartment. They did not embrace as they said goodbye.

Her gaze never left her father, the screaming never ceased. That was a problem, she had seen his face and seen the money. This all could be solved by easing the girl's pain. The thought repulsed Charles somewhat, causing a physical wince and a hard swallowing action. In the end he just walked away.

Lights inside nearby apartments flickered on as Charles hobbled away from the blaring screams of a girl who had lost everything. A less cynical man would worry that these neighbours would come to the aid of the girl and in the process stop his escape, but Charles knew that no one would. They all just watch and listen, assume someone else will be the hero.

Maybe when this is all over, when the guilt is too much and he know Jane is safe; maybe he will return. Maybe the little girl, no longer little, will rally these bystanders and those close to her father, and they will rip him apart. Then they will both be at peace. That may be his tomorrow but on this day Charles's priority was getting home, getting in contact with that psycho and getting Jane back. These were Charles's thoughts as he made his way home.

No one double takes at the sight of a bloody beaten man dragging along a bag of money, at least not a bloody beaten man with a gun in his other hand. No one said anything when he gets on the Rail, no one said anything when he gets off. No one said anything when he passes out in the hall.

-BRRRRIIIIINNNNG!-

Thick flakes of dried blood fall out of his nose and ears. He grabs the phone. More blood on his hands. He doesn't bother saying hello. Charles know it's him.

"Do you have the money?"

"Almost all of it."

"Almost isn't good enough."

The pain ripped through him, shock set in before the gunshot could be registered; the gunshot then the scream.

The phone went dead.

The shock blocked the agony of the previous moments, how he longed for it. Charles knew he deserved that agony. Instead adrenaline rushed through his veins, he didn't know what to do. He threw himself against his mess of belongings; cabinets and bookcases, anything harder than himself. Finally after minutes of self-destruction he smashed his head against a mirror, then he was gone.

The blood flowed from him, he wished that he could have just laughed at the absurdity, the brutality and the veracity. Just drift into a haze of delusion and fantasy until starvation laid him to waste. He suspected that he could never let himself die, not by his own doing. Though he possessed intimate knowledge of the methods and avoidable mistakes involved in suicide. He lacked a certain commitment to the unknown. Perhaps he could let himself starve or dehydrate. The gangsters would likely find him before such events could begin to occur.

In the end Charles called the police. Police aren't exactly what they used to be, they are privately operated and act mostly as henchmen for sectors of the government. They do on occasion take tips. Got to stay busy somehow.

Charles knew the state would kill him, he just thought it would be a cleaner death.

His shaky bloody fingers dialled the number, he told them someone was storing stolen government medical supplies at his address.

Charles took a quarter of the money from the bag, he knew he wouldn't need it now. The Police would take the rest. He placed the credits in a separate bag and entered Claire's apartment. Charles sprawled a letter addressed to Claire, explaining all that had transpired, that the money was theirs and that he would likely soon be dead.

Their apartment was almost as messy as Charles's. He didn't have long and needed to find a hiding spot. It wasn't exactly Sherlock Holmes work but Charles placed the bag behind the gas line then switched it off. Claire would find it the next time she attempted cooking. Knowing Claire, Charles figured it may be weeks but she would find it.

He then sat on the dirt ridden floor of what soon would never be his apartment again. The floorboards creaked under his weight, the boards damp yet somehow incredibly dusty. He supposed prison would be worse, he struggled to comprehend how but some things you just know.

Charles didn't hear the door burst open, didn't see shards of wood tearing through the smoke as the Kevlar garbed squad stormed in. He didn't feel the fists, batons and boots tear through him. Just the cracking of ribs, then waking up hours later, caged.

The sun was not shining so brightly when Jane awoke from her comfortable slumber, though the City was more than beautiful enough. The Charming Man set her up with an apartment on the 25th floor of a 27 floor building in the centre of Sector 5. He stopped by twice a week, they would go out, drink and see a show. Then sleep in the next day. She was unsure as to whether they were an item. He knew she fancied him but never knew if theirs was a romantic relationship. Though now that she was living in the City it was true to say that he was her entire world, she was not allowed out of the building without him. Jane's identification was still being processed.

It wasn't so bad, there was a pool, a gym, a library and even a television. Looking upon the city was always the best way to kill time. Jane began to paint the occasional landscape, still lives of the various streets visible from her window.

One particular night, The Charming Man took Jane to the most extravagant of parties. The *Benevolence Ball*. Oh, how she always wished to be whisked away to such an event. All the dresses, all the dancing. The Charming Man took her by the arm as they entered a magnificent grand hall. He kissed her and spoke sweet words in her ear,

"Come my Angel."

The structure seemed to be constructed from a dark stone, possibly basalt, and golden statues of men who Jane did not recognise basked in the entry. As he took Jane's hand, they descended into a rainbow of colour and music.

He wore a maroon suit, with a pale golden pocket square to match her dress. Many faces turned towards them as they made their way to the centre of the hall. Their attention did not amount to conversion. Not for quite some time. The Charming Man took Jane by the waist as the music slowed down, they swayed against one another; Jane overtly aware of her hearts strong beats. They remained that way until after hours of dancing a stunning blonde woman approached Jane. Her red dress, clung to her splendour frame, in a near beautiful way. Near.

Her words were slurred slightly and she spoke with an eccentric foreign accent. She addressed Jane as the *New Girl*, Jane blushed at the association. She asked so many questions, pausing as she thought of new enquiries. Jane showed her, the tag on her arm and they discussed what life was like in The Jungle. She seemed particularly curios about the dirty T.V and the dirtier people.

Jane had not spoken to the Charming Man in a matter of hours. He had been off talking to various business associates, he also accepted an award for outstanding achievement in something. It isn't completely relevant, Jane just cheered and applauded.

Some more food was served by buzzing drones. It tasted fantastic but Jane had indulged a little too much and made sure to limit herself.

The blonde woman's partner arrived. He had long black hair and a well-trimmed beard, his suit was dark in the classic manner, he was young and he spoke confidently with what would have once been considered a Salisbury accent. He reminded Jane of what Charlie used to be and what he might have been. He was a surgeon too after all, plastic surgery. He told Jane of all the plastic woman walking about the room, the cows that they had once been. He gave Jane his card, it took her a bit a back. Sensing her discomfort, he followed up with the line;

"No one is perfect, not yet at least."

Jane found her way to the balcony which overlooked the rest of the city, the stairs were sharp and steep but she managed, even in her altered state and the six inch heels. The Charming Man arrived their minutes later.

The two embraced, he held her as she looked upon the city lights, you couldn't see the horizon due to the walls, but who would want to see that dirty sprawl of building and whores with loose morals?

He held her for quite some time and he spoke affectionately the words "you are mine." Jane had been waiting to hear those words, or something similar, for so long. As he let go she told him that he was hers, but she turned to find him already descending back into the hall.

Jane stayed there for quite some time. The lights of the city were wonderful and vibrant, though something in Jane longed for the concealing darkness which she knew existed, her mind drifted towards Charlie. Did he miss her? Probably, she just hoped he was happy for her and happy for himself.

Jane heard cheers coming from the hall as a drone carrying glasses of champagne found its way to her. She took three. Drank them as quickly as possible. Then her worries drifted away.

Everything went smoothly until she broke her heel on the way down the stairs, there was a loud thud and many eyes found themselves to be fixated upon her, then the erupted into a thunder of laughter. Jane laughed as well, until her eyes met his gaze. He excused them shortly thereafter.

That was the first night it began.

The Jungle Correctional Facility, affectionately dubbed the *zoo* by its inhabitants was located below the streets of Sector 12. The more secure location among the animals. Charles shared his new residence with eighty-seven other *gentleman*. No woman. Curious. Charles supposed there was another Facility for woman; would it be called the Jungle Correctional Facility for Woman? Or was it just a separate part of the structure. He came to the conclusion that it didn't particularly matter.

The low head-count was due to the great efficiency that sentencing without any form of trial brings. Death in 60 days, maybe less. Charles did not receive the information from a judge or representative of whatever replaced the justice system. The colossus of a guard informed him, in a monotone eastern European accent, as he pushed Charles into his closet of a cell. Just a blanket and a small hole in the corner.

The guard couldn't have been older than seventeen, his skin pale, with the occasional blemish. In the goliaths hand a large steel bucket. Once Charles was firmly committed to the ground, the two made eye contact. The boy made sure of it. The contents of the bucket were then cast upon Charles. A cloud of glistening white powder descended. Charles would smell it, before he felt it, but once he felt it, it would not stop. The bubbles burnt his hair off, eyelashes and all. Leaving him an agonising mess, his flesh tender, having lost many vital layers.

The guard just stood there and watched. Charles supposed that maybe he knew, as well as he that this was the hell Charles deserved.

Charles's father, was a criminal prosecutor. He sent many men and woman to jail. In Charles's youth he enquired of him as to whether this saddened his father, did it bring with it some sense of guilt? He told his son: "No, we send them there in the hope that they may one day get better." Charles would not be getting better. The guise of rehabilitation was given up long ago, replaced only by grim and swift punishment. Charles knew they would kill him but the first few weeks he wished that they would simply hurry up about it.

Each day was excruciating. The regiment consisted of a nutritious gruel breakfast laced with various poisons and no doubt pesticides. Then five hours of hard labour, then lunch laced with the same agony. It made your throat, stomach and almost everything else burn and pulsate. Wither but never die. Not for a lack of trying. Charles observed many of his illustrious peers attempt such a task. He had only been there a week when he first observed the phenomenon. A man of great stature walked through the hall and asked for the lunches of others. Charles had imagined that the man would have sported an impressive set of facial hair before he was imprisoned. One by one they gave him their lunch, some men cheered. How perplexing. Cheering for a suicide. Cheering for an agonising end to an already painful existence.

It did not end with the dark painless silence which the inmates craved. Just ecstatic agony, just shrieks of horrid torture.

After these festivities, the inmates were sent for *treatment*. A terribly unimaginative alias for torture. The others informed Charles that these tortures were different for each of them. Preying on whatever fibres of humanity they had left, like sticking a finger in an open wound so it will never heal. Charles's treatment involved flashing images of Jane. All throughout her life. Many of the pictures came from the apartment they had shared, others Charles had never lay eyes on. Figures of her father and other nameless family that all shared her reflective eyes. Each image was then followed by a powerful electric convulsion then an injection of some unknown stimulant. In honesty it destroyed him, but it was a deep and singular solitude to see her face flash before him. He would scream, he would cry, but not all of his tears would be for them.

Then Charles was left in his dark empty cell, to dwell. Cramped alongside his own lamentations. First his thoughts drifted to the young girl, he thought of all the ways in which she would have lost. He wished he could take it back, though he knew such thoughts were futile. Then he allowed himself to think of his own fate. To dwell on his impending and unavoidable death. Charles had always in his deepest thoughts been driven by a base fear of death, though now, in this place he almost welcomed the promise. Finally Charles's thoughts drifted to Jane, the many years they had together, the many more that had been robbed from him; how he loved her. How he failed her.

It had been several weeks since the last of The Charming Man's visits. It did not bring Jane happiness, though she wished it did not bring her so much despair. He had struck out at her unexpectedly. They had arrived at her home and he had thrown her against the wall. Lifting her so that her legs found themselves wrapped around him, he undressed her. Ran his soft hands down her long spine, Jane had expected something different. Instead she found herself at the bottom of her stair case. Alone.

Left to sulk by herself. The weather sulking along with her. Miserable rain pouring down, taunting her, ruining her view of the city. All of the paintings that she had so enthusiastically began were thrown aside, waiting until the weather cleared up once more.

Finding herself bored and near out of her mind, Jane picked up a book for the first time in a few years. It was a miserable tale about the exploits of some stupid poxy boy. She only read the first few chapters before tossing it. "I bet Charlie would have enjoyed it," she couldn't help but think that somehow books such as that did not contain any hidden insight into the world, but people find meaning in anything.

This had always been her approach to art. The subjectivity of meaning. She had once made a living painting silhouette skylines and mountainsides, existing only on the folds of her imagination. Jane had first met Charlie at her own art exhibition, he had come to support a friend and as the night drifted on he approached her and made two offers, the first regarding a large canvas painting, the second regarding a date with her. And so their love affair began, with swift and ecstatic motion. Too bad it had ended so stagnant.

For a long while she passed the time by tearing apart some of her clothes and re-stitching them together, creating new and different pieces of clothing. It was messy and clumsy but the occasional item made an impression.

It was a Thursday evening when he returned, his hand empty, his suit white and gold; freshly pressed. He did not knock, he opened the door with a key Jane had no knowledge of. She found him on the couch.

"How dare you?"

She screeched at him. A look of confused bemusement, then etched upon his face. He tilted his head and his perfect blue eyes turned to a squint.

"How dare I, what?"

He explained to her that she had fallen due to her own inebriation that he had stayed with her all night, but had to leave in the morning for working commitments. She did not buy it at first, though her recollection was hazy. Jane did not entirely trust his version of events. Though what reason would he have to lie. She was his to do whatever he wanted, she wouldn't be able to even leave the building without him. He pointed towards a scuff mark on the wall. Jane vaguely remembered her foot catching the wall before she plummeted.

The Charming Man moved to stand beside her. She was hesitant at first but she allowed him to run his hand down her back. Goosebumps guiding the way. It felt awkward and painful at first but his hands began to massage and knead her spine. Soon all the pain melted away. She smiled, he smiled back. Neither knew entirely were they stood with one another, though Jane felt that she had incorrectly lashed out at him, some guilt and an unshakable suspicion lingered within her.

They ate dinner in a café, two streets away. It was dark and orchestral music played dull in the background. Jane ordered soup. It seemed the appropriate dish for such weather, though she found it to be less than appetising. For a long time neither of them exchanged words. Eventually the Charming Man told her where he had been the last few weeks. In the Desert, building living facilities for the outcasts and crazy people.

Then he asked Jane if she would wish to meet him during his next trip. He would be inspecting various Epsilon facilities, he asked whether she would wish to meet him in Sector 23.

"How would I do that?"

Her answer came out with confusion, peppered with undertones of annoyance. If The Charming Man was taken aback by this he did not show it. He simply produced a small black book from the folds of his jacket. Handing it to Jane, she opened to find; *Jane Clements/Sector 5 resident.* With this document she would be able to travel and see the city. The two embraced. They walked back towards the apartment hand in hand. In an odd way she had never felt closer to him. Jane phoned Claire to say she would be visiting soon.

Charles's hair never grew back, at least nowhere of much notability. Though they were all that way. Hairless, stripped of their humanity walking hand in hand towards the grave, together, monstrosities.

Contact with other inmates was quite limited, though Charles did eventually strike up a friendship with a man who went by the title of Weasel. He was a scrawny and tall man with a strangely thin face. Weasel was on charges of theft, he was caught stealing government supplies to save the needy in his Sector. Charles eventually enquired as to his name, he told him its personnel etymology originated as an insult other children would use to make fun of his untidy appearance, he was halfway through gesturing to his non-existent unruly hair, before he realised. Weasel like many children took the name for himself so that it would never hurt as badly. Weasel was a bright guy, and he left quite an impression on Charles. A rare soul, as pure a nature as one could have in such a world.

Most days they would labour and eat together, swapping stories and misremembering jokes. Weasel often would pass on pieces of information, rumours and such. He had been in the facility for two months before Charles arrived. In this time he had lost close to twenty kilograms, it wasn't the exercise, more likely a terrible combination of the food and the fear of the place. It was eating Charles up inside but he had little within himself, he figured he should have been numb to it. Weasel had a family, a family and a Sector who he had stolen from the government to save. Charles did not deserve to make his acquaintance. Even though Charles refused to tell him of his crimes, Weasel still accepted him. A good and beautiful man despite the ugliness which engulfed him. For a time Charles believed that he himself would remain above the desolation but he had succumbed. Weasel would die a good man.

Charles mulled over this as they were instructed to dig a hole. The tools given to them primitive and the ground rocky and barren. A guard was screaming the entire time. Quite inspirational. Weasel kept digging, continued to try, Charles lagged behind but they got it done. Five hours of work. Then they filled it in, right in front of them. Charles cursed at the wind. Weasel just stood there. Quiet, straight backed, confident. Charles felt himself to be Sisyphus, Weasel was closer to Christ.

Guards seized Charles on his way back to his cell. Powerful arms dragging him through the painfully white corridors, until finally they arrived at a room Charles had never before seen. The guards gestured at the door, they did not follow him in.

The inside was the same horrific white, a large room divided by a glass wall. Claire stood unexpectedly in front of Charles. They stood apart for a long time. Claire, sizing him up, attempting to find anything resembling the human that he had once been, Charles on the other hand stood confused and worried for her safety. She gestured to come closer, he obliged. Claire then proceeded to lift up her shirt. Her breasts exposed, her nipples cracked, the kind of war torn that comes with a needy child. In honesty, it took Charles a few seconds to notice the message sprawled across her chest.

Jane alive, visiting in two weeks.
Come back next week to
Pass on a message

She moved against the glass in a pseudo sexual manner, only then did he notice the guard standing twelve feet behind. Claire blew a kiss, asked if he missed "them", then finally gave a mournful smile as she made herself proper and existed the room.

The adrenaline of the recent discovery coursed through Charles. He did not feel the guard's strikes as he was berated back to his cell. His thoughts frenzied and scattered as he attempted to comprehend this most recent realisation. Was Jane responsible, for these occurrences? Was she in league with that thing? He doubted it, instead he chose to believe that she was another victim, perhaps in more danger then himself. Yet still the thought, that she may have done this to him, stayed, unshakable and resolute.

Jane spent hours upon hours scouring the streets of the Outer City. Alone the world took a different shade, darker, empty, though nonetheless interesting. It had only recently dawned upon her how empty these streets were. So few had so much.

Jane's back had finally healed and she was ready to travel once more, she would be meeting The Charming Man in Sector 23 soon. She was just killing time in a dull little café in Sector 8. The tea was nice but it lacked a certain ambience, found beyond Sector 6. She toyed with the last of her carrot cake as she thought over what possibilities lay ahead. If Charlie was still around she would find him. Make things right. Perhaps The Charming Man would be able to help him financially. She wanted him to be happy. He deserved to be happy and perhaps he would find happiness without her.

Jane's line of thought was interrupted by the arrival of a slim figure with beady eyes and short knotted hair. He was one of The Charming Mans employees. A rather dull man, he rarely spoke and when he did Jane wished he didn't; his teeth were abhorrent. He led her out to the street. A white luxury car was waiting for us. White. The colour seemed curious. All the others had been the same regimental black. Perhaps this would be her permanent car. She only hoped that this would not be her permanent driver.

Jane's bags were stacked in the back, she brought two. One of which was filled with silk and cotton dresses for Claire. Jane thought Claire deserved something beautiful. After all Jane felt poorly that she would not be there to give Claire the help she had previously.

The sectors beyond the outer wall looked far more terrible than Jane had remembered. Charlie always spoke of the urban decay. Only now it was real. Jane wondered what had transpired in her absence. The driver did not answer when she asked where exactly they were going. She shouldn't have been surprised when they arrived in Sector 23.

The driver opened the door and simply said,

"He is waiting."

The worlds seeped from his skinny beak of a mouth.

Jane passed a group of young tramps on her way up. Their childish conversations extinguished by her presence. Maybe she would inspire the vicious sluts. Change them, show them that they can be something more. They probably couldn't and they probably wouldn't recognise her either.

Once she arrived on the top floor she approached the two doors. Jane had planned to go through both, but which first. The sound of a baby stirring lead her into Claire's apartment. The Charming Man seated on what appeared to be a new couch, holding Simon in his arms. The pair were smiling, their eyes interlocked. Until they saw Jane at least. Claire greeted her first and The Charming Man passed on the baby as to embrace her.

The following conversation was awkward and long. Claire's jealousy seeped through and poisoned the discussion. Charlie was not mentioned. Eventually the skinny driver brought the bag up and Claire went through all of the nice things Jane had bought. Not even a smile. Just awkward staggered grimaces. Jane felt as if she could have cried.

As if sensing this, The Charming Man excused them, they made a hollow embrace, and Claire made Jane promise to return in a week. She said yes but had little intention of following through. The pair walked into the hall. Jane stared at the door behind which her previous life was once held. She could almost feel Charlie's presence, seeping from within. He didn't want to talk to her.

Back in the car, they returned to their life.

Living conditions had not been improving for Charles. His right arm had become infected and each shovel load burned through him. Weasel was picking up the ever increasing slack that Charles was creating. The 'treatments' were getting worse. The drugs now significantly stronger. The pictures, distressing. Images of Jane in her teenage years. Unnaturally thin, a needle sticking in her arm, her eyes glazed. The photos would send shivers down his spine, even without the stimulants and the electricity. The dosage had increased as a result of his system adapting to the poison. It left him convulsing at night. At breakfast the spoon never quite found its way to his mouth. He lost most of the slight strength which he had left. The guards continued their assaults upon him. They were not as brutal in nature as they had been prior to his now overly weakened state. The assaults were precise and subtle, though none the less agonising. Thin blades forced beneath fingernails and chemical sprays forced into his lungs became his tortured routine.

Charles's sanity was his only possession. Though the legitimacy of this sanity could have been easily questioned. He would see things. A mix of sleep deprivation and lack of nutrition was resulting in hallucinations. Old memories of Jane. Some of these memories occurred, such as what Jane looked like when they first met, their first date, their first kiss, and the first time they made love. Though some of the hallucinations would never occur; Charles saw fleeting images of Jane in a beautiful wedding dress, their first child. He wished these images would stay in frame for longer, the second he focused upon them, they evaporated.

Though the memories of a life that could have been stayed with him. Once these memories would have destroyed him. Rip the fibres of his being apart. Though somehow, Charles found a way to use these false memories to steel himself to the hell around him. It was not much, not enough to sustain him forever. Though luckily he did not have forever. No one really does but plenty forget that often enough. Charles remembered years of his life when the concept of mortality never once crossed his mind. Not his own at least. Those years of drink and study. The world was his and he would do everything to make it a better place. It was a strange egoism, though his intentions were always close to the right place. In the recesses of Charles's mind he always questioned his own sincerity. The world was filled with *wanttobe* saviours born with silver spoons in their mouths. Though the day after his long awaited graduation was spent in a dark and messy clinic, preforming much needed surgeries to young immigrants. After a year, his skill became undeniable. Offers flooded in from various hospitals. Charles took up a position at The People's Hospital of London. He was earning ten times what he had previously, he donated the difference to the clinic, allowing for three more doctors, refurbishment of the emergency room and a full time cleaner.

It was around this time Charles and Jane first met. A few years later The Union took power. The Ryan's had enough money to secure themselves, though Charles would have no part in it. He stayed behind with Jane, spending whatever he could on medical supplies. His first clinic was destroyed by the government within the first month. His second was raided by gangs three months later. Leaving only enough gauze to shield his broken eye socket from the sun.

Much of what Charles had been was left behind in those months. Jane had helped him through. Though even love does begin to wane. Now Charles found himself staring into the darkness of a soon to be filled in hole. He had liked to think that some part of his essence drifted too her, but he remained stationary. It was just him, Weasel and the pit. Together they finished the hole off. Together they watched the hole be filled in. Charles examined Weasel as the grains of earth fell to the ground. Never did he wince, or show pain or hatred, even dissatisfaction would be found absent. Something in Charles knew that he could never be what he had wished. He was defeated years before he was ever born. Perhaps in a simpler time he could have made a difference, but not in The Jungle.

That afternoon, the guards as usual tried their hardest to get Charles to fight back so that they would feel obliged to put the prisoner in his place. Though Charles would not budge, they beat him anyway. The Treatment began. Though the drugs and he electricity was poisoning his body, Charles's mind stayed with the image of Jane. On their wedding day. It would never happen, but to Charles in those moments it didn't matter.

The City was ablaze with their return. Their first evening back was spent at a large party in a Sector 5 apartment. By this time people were beginning to learn Jane's name. She was wearing a dark blue dress, mostly silk, though some satin mixed through to create a darker pattern. The Charming Man would arrive later in the evening. Jane's driver sat inside the car parked on the street. Every now and then, Jane walked toward the window to see if he was still there. She had told him to go somewhere else while she was inside. Though there he remained. It was beginning to unnerve her. She forced herself to make conversation with the other guests as a means to keep her mind from the eerie man in the car.

Eventually Jane found the young surgeon and his girlfriend. The three sat down at a table in the middle of the apartment. The girlfriend was again wearing a red dress. This one significantly shorter, less formal but still as extravagant. She was beautiful. Though, surely her boyfriend helped to create this effect. The two were curious about Jane's trip back to the Jungle. She told them about Claire and her jealousy. They expressed their sympathy. The girlfriend told Jane about jealous friends that she had had before The Union took over. They told her that it wasn't her fault, and that Jane would do best to put the Jungle behind her. More alcohol was consumed. The surgeon and the girlfriend both took a few pills. The music turned up and the three of them began to dance. Conversation usually impossible after a certain hour.

The three stayed near each other but joined a much larger group. The body heat and alcohol caused Jane to sweat and for a moment she considered undressing. Though The Charming Man would arrive soon, she did not wish to embarrass him. Instead she made her way to a balcony and sat down outside. Feeling tired, overheated and somewhat nauseas. Jane fell asleep.

The Charming Man finally arrived at the party. Men and women greeted him. He was wearing a dark green satin smoking jacket with grey pants. His white shirt unbuttoned at the neck. His tie removed, now lingering in the folds of his coat. He walked to the window to see if Jane's driver had removed himself, he had. After a few minutes of searching. The Charming Man found Jane asleep on the balcony. He pressed his hand against her arm. She awoke suddenly. Her hand snapped defensively at him. When she realised what she had done she looked embarrassed. For a long time they sat with each other. His hand on her leg, her hands grasping on her arm. The night air was cold on her skin but she did not want to return inside. Only when the party was wrapping up did they return. To say final goodbyes and organise future social encounters.

They walked to his car. The drive to her apartment was not far, though Jane began to feel car sick, making the journey feel significantly longer. Jane reached to find The Charming Man's hand, though it had been absently placed in his lap. To reach that far would be awkward and it appeared that he did not notice. So she settled for rolling down the window a crack as to access the night air.

When they arrived at the apartment. Jane made her way to the bathroom. Perched over the toilet. She was dry reaching for a few minutes before she returned to the bedroom. The Charming man was lying in bed, already undressed. Jane folded her dress and placed it on the sideboard before joining him. She tried to fall to sleep but the nausea made such prospects impossible. She moved towards him, wrapping an arm around his shoulder blades, resting her head on his chest. At first he held her. Then his hands descended towards her breasts. She tried to nudge him off. Though he was adamant. Eventually he gave up and the two laid apart, just barely feeling whatever warmth was left.

The piece of paper exclaiming the date of Charles's execution arrived to him at breakfast. Conveniently it came before his meeting with Claire. Inconveniently he had already written his response. There is no white out for text written in laceration.

Charles approached Weasel about it in the yard. He had already known about his correspondence. He had sourced Charles the blade, it was dull and a little blunt but it did the job. Weasel refused to do it for him the first time. He said he was squeamish. Charles had once thought the same about himself. That was before he ripped the life out of another human being. So ripping through himself wasn't so bad.

Weasel agreed to write the correction

Get away from him

~~Don't visit~~

I love you

Come to my Execution

Week from today

Please

In a sick way it reminded him of high school, sitting over his tablet trying to figure out how to cut thousands of words into one simple omnipotent paragraph. Weasel vomited into their Sisyphus pit. Charles's stomach churned, not at the sight of the emesis, more that the vomit looked utterly indistinguishable from the meals which he received.

The same guard came and found him, they arrived at the same room, he didn't abuse Charles this time. He patted him on the back and said with what seemed like all the sympathy he could manage; "Just don't get your knob out."

Charles felt that he could almost smile, though the task was too taxing. Claire was again on the other side of the glass. She again gestured for him to come forth. Charles obliged, lifted his shirt. She winced. He told her that he would be dead soon. That he wanted her to be happy. After he was sure she had committed it to memory Charles walked away.

The guards didn't touch him for the remaining days. Courtesy, he suspected.

Charles wondered where these guards were sourced, they were slaves like himself and the others but perhaps in a stricter sense. Maybe they sold their souls. Or maybe they are victims too. It reminded him of a few studies he had once read. Students placed as guards and prisoners. It all went well for the first twelve hours, then the torture began. He wondered who was more terrible the guards or himself.

Weasel got his slip a few days later. In most ways Charles felt worse for him then he did for himself. Though like all saints of veracious biblical proportion, Weasel took his sentence without the shed of a tear. He smiled quite frequently. It was almost alarming how hard he worked, the sweat he shed digging those pits. Charles mostly sat about and moped around, beating his fist against the ground and crying out at this fucked up world. They had given up on the treatment. In spare moments Charles obscured the message he would leave behind. He drew. Carved new letters over the top. Now he would appear insane in the crazy sense, rather than the truer sense.

On Charles's last day on this earth he ate the same poisoned foods, dug the same hole. Then finally a brake form the horrific normalcy. He was given an hour of alone time. Weasel could not follow him into the empty room, the two shook hands, and both men held a mournful gaze. A solitary tear slid down the pale granite of Charles's expression as he entered the room. Charles figured it was just another form of torture. The empty room served no purpose other than to allow for all the unease and panic to bubble to the surface.

Eventually a guard walked in. Charles recognised him in an instant. It was the first of them. The young one. He told Charles to get up. There was something in that tone. Charles would never know exactly what snapped in him, but something sure did.

Charles took the cowards route, he allowed the guard to turn his back. Kicking hard at the back of his knees the boy collapsed, Charles's hands covering the boy's mouth. Charles placed the blade inside the boy's check. Then he beat him, the blood poured out of his mouth. He screamed and others were soon on top of Charles. The sedative took hold.

Charles awoke to a room of dark grey, needles and tubes stuck in his neck and wrists. A doctor with platinum blonde hair was observing him. She spoke in a foreign accent,

"It's time."

The curtain in front of Charles opened; revealing the last face he would ever see.

The Charming Man and Jane had not been getting along since the day they returned home, he had stayed with her every night since. Things had begun to become rather agitated. Each night she would feel the weight of the bed change as he left. His phone ever-present, always in communication with business associates. He only had time for dinner, drinks and other such pleasantries. She was beginning to get sick of it so on the sixth night she approached him. It was a mistake, he simply told her that it "Wasn't her concern." That cold remark sent Jane into hysterics. Her tears met with nothing but an icy vacant stare. Her reaction to this was not quite so measured. She tossed a large ceramic serving plate, her exact target was unclear, though the shards and white powder landed inches from his fine leather shoes. The awe never struck him, he did not freeze in place. He proceeded towards Jane with more purpose and brutality of figure than she had ever witnessed. The first strike was expected, an open handed slap across the face. She froze. Then the backhand which forced her to the ground. Jane lay there crying, her mouth bleeding. He proceeded to make his calls.

Dawn came and Jane found herself still stuck to the floor. Something inside her missed Charles severely. Finally realising the scope of her mistakes. The Charming Man absent, she proceeded down the stairs. Her white car and its disgusting driver were waiting. Take me to Sector 23. He nodded and they began their journey.

It was a lovely day and in a strange way she was both scared and optimistic. Maybe Charles would take her back? The Charming Man didn't seem to want her anymore. Maybe Charles could beat up her brute of a driver and they would sell the car to one of the gangs. It was fanatic but it seemed possible.

The car pulled up, she was so lost in thought, she didn't realise the shortness of the journey. She opened the door of the car, revealing the *Sector 12 Hotel*. The driver was quickly at her lateral. "He's waiting inside". She didn't need to ask where.

He was sitting on the bed when she walked inside. The driver followed behind. Standing at the door. He began to smoke, averting his eyes, trying not to acknowledge Jane's existence. The Charming Man was wearing a white shirt, open at the neck with the sleeves rolled up.

No one spoke. The room silent, it was agonising. Jane began to cry. It distorted and weakened her words making them seem childish,

"I thought I was special."

His reply was simplistic and harshly cruel
"No."
He produced a box from beneath the bed, then placed a note on top. Then he began to walk out the door, before he left he turned to her, took her left hand and spoke,
"Take your time, I will be waiting for you outside."
The driver remained.
The box was made from beautiful, fragrant wood, covered in a red finish. Placing the note aside, she delved inside. The box contained a bottle of expensive champagne, pre chilled, bottles of makeup, various pieces of gold and diamond jewellery, lastly and most prominently a dress. It was the most beautiful thing she had ever seen. White silk in a wedding like style. She smiled, reaching for the note, all happiness was swept away.
The note in Claire's hand writing read
10/08/78. Charles on trial for murder. Set up by that rich psycho, he is being held in the Sector 12 Jail, this is his message to you:

Get away from him

I love you

Come to my Execution

Week from today

Please

It was the 17th of August. She dropped to her knees in despair as she looked through the window, out into the light blue clear sky. The driver moved closer, his feet heavier than possible for a man so small.
He dropped a four meter length of rope on the ground next to her. The Charming Man's words rang through the girls head;
"Come my Angel."

Footnote

It wasn't my finest work. Some complications got in the way of things, though Weasel and my friends in the city played their parts rather well, I do believe. Though I must continue. Continue the great experiment that is life. For what is the world without angels?

This is how I have once again found myself in another dark and crowded bar. Not as bad as the last but a few too many bodies for my taste. I find myself nursing my second drink, as the subtle art of my performance requires complete commitment. I have watched and waited, finally spotting my target. A new friend perhaps. She has long legs and strawberry blonde hair, sitting with a boyfriend or husband. I recognise him from a factory a few Sectors south of here. I must remember to pull his file when I return home.

He, from the looks of him, does not seem all that bright, not like the last one. Not as pathetic either. Thinking back to the rage and disgrace Charles felt when he realised I would be the solitary figure to watch him die. This new one won't likely be as fun.

The man is making his way towards the bathroom, alone the girl appears void of the innocence I had noticed in her the day before. Up close in the streets of Sector 12 she had possessed a certain rare elegance. We can only hope this will return, as our relationship progresses. None the less I am certain she will make a wonderful angel; a stunning bride.

Part II:

The Games We Play

Well-dressed bodies moved and writhed against each other in rhythm to the rhythm-less beat of horrendous electronic music. The *Benevolence Ball* was a yearly event, where the citizens of Sector 2 through to Sector 8 dug deep into their silk lined pockets, to produce the necessary credits to fund the preservation of the City's outer walls, and any other such 'necessary infrastructure'. How gallant, how gracious, how pure of these private citizens to fund public assets.

The event began three hours earlier; as well dressed men and woman arrived at the Sector 3 *Union Hall*. An impressive structure, the first of two Union buildings within the *City*. Both looked as if carved out of the world's largest block of basalt, adorned with statues of various Kings and Queens of old. No one recognises a face but they are all proud none the less. The most impressive statue stood at the entrance of the hall, depicting King George III shaking hands with Henry Ford. Neither man had breathed the same air, more than a century dividing them. No one questions it. Not in a society of free market capitalist, aristocrat slaves.

Soon the hall is packed with well pampered women, all dressed in similar intricate, bulky, colourful dresses; reminiscent of birds of paradise. Accompanying them, men in near uniform black suits and silk black ties. Political businessman, inventors, actors and other such well-regarded public figures. All of them making light chit-chat. Conversations all vaguely related to sex and/or money. Exotic foods and expensive alcohols are passed around. People eat and drink, pretend they are happy.

Watching all of this is the Chairmen, a fat, old dandy and the Union's official representative in the Kingdoms. He doesn't speak, just watches; watches all these money whores pretend that they're free. Pretend the Union doesn't get half. Maybe that's why we all drink so much, to forget. The drugs don't come out for hours but when they do; there is no stopping it. The music becomes louder, inhibitions lost in the cadence. Some men and women disrobe, most don't. The party rages on. Who knew altruism could be so much fun?

I suppose this is the point in the narrative where, I, your narrator, am obliged to introduce myself. Say who I am, why I am, spill my guts about how mother hit me. All that crap. I would prefer not. My name is Harry Neals (its polish or something). I am the *Senior Minister of Offence* at *Epsilon*

Incorporated. No that does not mean my job revolves around snarky remarks and blatant insults, though it does seem an inadvertent, encompassing aspect of my work.

In our government system, each business provides something essential to the upkeep and continuation of society. Whatever business provides the most, holds the most power. Competition means less power, less power means less money. Less money is a problem. This is where I and people like me come in. Through espionage, extortion and murder we create monopolies. Dynasties. Of course no one knows me as *Harry the Hit-Man*, though, that handle has quite the ring to it. Most know me as *Harry the Vice Transport Minister*. It's boring and no one asks relevant questions.

On this day, like the other whores, I am here on business. My target, Maxwell Fisher, the C.E.O of a medium sized start up based in Sector 26. Producing sustainable energy for the surrounding factories. This is a problem because, as of yesterday, Epsilon owns a three hundred square kilometre nuclear power facility. So naturally Mr Fisher has to be eliminated. Fisher was a smaller than average man, with above average ambitions and the intellect to back it up. Initially we tried recruitment. His rejection catalysed his death. He was always going to die. One way or another. He just accelerated the process. Fisher like most of the City's population had a rather unhealthy love of drugs. When I caught up with him, he was deprived of his pants, being helped into a car by a paid bodyguard.

I followed him to his apartment in Sector 4. My driver picked me up and dropped me at the building. As *'Transport Minister'* I don't need to stop between sectors. The building was small and held only two apartments. The building itself designed by some nameless artist. It was intricate and the schematics were difficult, though lucky for me the Security Minister is a dear friend. The algorithm unlocked the front door in less than a second.

I walked down the empty hall. Though the building only held two tenants the hall was filled with unusual romantic era paintings. It was humorous to imagine the two residents discussing the vibe they wished to present, then departing one another to live in their separate empty apartments. Fisher however, was not alone. The light shone out of the crack below his front door. Mahogany, unstained, real lock. Was probably an aesthetic choice. I used one of a thousand possible implements to get it unlocked. I took the dart gun out of my jacket pocket. The grip, the weight of it; it always felt right. It was ergonomically designed for me, though each use felt like an exciting surprise of unmeasurable comfort. The soles of my shoes made no sound as I entered into the unreasonably large living room. Chandeliers hung from each corner, each ornamented with various rare jewels. The low sustained hum of snoring filled the room, a toilet flushed somewhere to my left. I took cover behind the kitchen island which separated myself and the bodyguard, zipping his fly with his somehow muscled fingers. I waited for him to pass before slipping out, I pressed the barrel into the folds of his neck.

"Go back into the bathroom, you found him like this."

I first pulled the weapon from his holster, replacing it with a thick roll of credits, making sure he felt the notes as they passed his ribs. I took a step back and lowered my arm, keeping the gun pointed at a ninety degree angle, he did not look back. I suspected this wasn't his first time. The less you know, I suppose.

I found Fisher lying face down on the bed, covered in his own vomit, a few of his veins had collapsed from over use. A bottle of scotch half empty on the bedside table. If I left him a few more hours he might have finished the job for me, but that wasn't really an option. I placed the needle between his fingers, felt the slightest of spasms as the cocktail entered his system. I returned the gun into its holster as I walked out into the night air. This was the cost of business in the City.

My driver dropped me off a few blocks from my building. The cold air of Sector 3 felt good against my skin. These walks were a regular vice of mine, frequently imagining the nefarious shadows that may linger around each bend. Rarely do my targets fulfil my need for such exhilaration. It's sad really, the way they just die, never do anything more than beg and barter, and that's the ones who realise what's happening, most will never see me coming. For most of those that do, the realisation never dawns in time.

I entered the building through the main lobby. My apartment sat on the third floor but it isn't the one I entered. The passageway required a precise tap on the dimple of the centre right brick of a modest yet decadent fireplace, located in the corner of the showroom apartment. This false apartment looked as if it had been well lived in, I ate my meals in it, hosted events in it regularly, made (what people falsely attribute to) love in it even more regularly; but never once had I laid my eyes to rest in it.

The opened passage led to my real home. A modest sized apartment, the main space consisted of only a bed and four three storey book cases, decorating the length of each wall. A small door sized passage way cut into each of the cases lead into a bathroom and wardrobe on the left and a vault on the right. The bathroom was almost the same size as the main room, brass fixtures and marble benches. The wardrobe consisted of five partitions: Inner City, for the delicate handmade suede suits and silk pocket squares, Outer City, nice designer cotton suits, Inner Jungle, crumpled jeans and jackets, Outer Jungle, torn and dirty shorts and shirts, and lastly the clothing of the Desert, its mostly obscure rags mixed with strange leathers of unknown origins. I laid down on the made bed and drifted into the ether.

Chapter 11

It was nearly 10am, the temperature was slowly lowering as winter began its approach. The C.E.O and Chancellor of Epsilon Incorporated sat across from myself, inside what would appear to outsiders and idiots as the Chancellor's office. Though this room like most others in this Sector 2 acropolis, was a fabrication. The desk is real mahogany, the picture on the table is his real wife, though the files on his computer and tablets are fabrications. Nothing kept in this room was indispensable. The Chancellor was a stout man with thin receding hair, his eyes bulbous and large, looking as if they could burst from the sockets if a sneeze even crossed his mind. He lay a file in front of me; manila. Inside, paper documents, printed on a typewriter. No data trail. The file would be in my hands for 48 hours before the ink would disappear and I was instructed to incinerate it as a precaution. The ink ribbon was already burned. The Chancellor did not speak for a time, waiting for me to make the first move. Perhaps he expected me to grab at the folder, snatch it away as to gloss over all the fun facts and figures, cost/benefit analyses and family histories, my home town and choice in pornography. I would not make the first move. We would sit there for quite some time, eye contact remaining steady. A glance down at his golden 20th century watch meant that he had lost. He sat up in his chair and spoke with a quiet intensity;

"What I ask of you today will require a great deal. Harry as of three hours ago you are no longer employed by Epsilon"

"How did that come to be?"

I spoke as my hand subconsciously drifted towards the holster behind my jacket breast.

"The story in common circulation will be that the transport department is reducing in size, that we really don't need a vice transport minister. However certain circles will be informed that your termination was due to indecent behaviour on your part, that you shagged the Minister for Agriculture's wife. You will be offered a job by Titan Enterprises by weeks end, their transport minister was found dead from a drug overdose. Appears it was legitimate. You are the practical candidate. They will also wish to extract whatever information they can from you"

He paused, as for me to take it all in.

"How did you know about me and Bernadette?"

The Chancellor did not find my joke amusing though we both knew it was not a joke.

"What I ask of you is highly unusual, it has never been attempted before and goes against many concords. Your job will be to destroy Titan from the inside. Everything you need to know is in that folder. A handler has been assigned to you, the two of you are quite familiar"

Before we progress, I should probably first explain a few things to you. As I stated earlier the government of my dear country is governed by many businesses, all of which attempt to provide diverging services, though more importantly these business's produce and rape the earth for whatever The Union needs. Epsilon and Titan are four of what was once ten major companies. These major companies always finding their way into destroying the smaller companies. Like so many nature films, bigger, meaner animals destroying the smaller ones. Then the big guys turned on one another, price wars flooded until finally a few years back Epsilon, Titan, Raine and Pinnacle conspired with one another and split production. Everyone remained fat and happy. Once the debt was paid these businesses would regain control over the nation. Now the Chancellor of Epsilon was asking me to help violate this agreement. I could not be more thrilled.

The Chancellor explained the plan briefly. Then he escorted me to my office. A room on the 30th floor. Three days a week I would sit at this desk, most hours spent exploring the vulgarities of my own mind or reading bad literature, though some time was spent memorising buzzwords and inferential statistics. Sometimes I thought I may have even learnt more than the so called experts around me. I was an actor, a snake, they were droning idiots. I opened the draws of my oak desk, then proceeded to close them, pausing and kneeling for good measure. Then as the final crescendo I lifted the solitary picture from my desk, my beautiful late wife. Elizabeth Hurley, 1965; lying on a beach in what was formally California. It was an arbitrary decision, I had not much enjoyed *The Sandpiper,* the film which the still is extracted. In truth I had much preferred Miss Hurley's portrayal of Cleopatra, though headdresses never made a formidable resurgence in fashion.

I found my now former employees lined up outside my office. Many of their dreary faces decorated with solitary tears. I shook their hands. Hugged the more attractive of the bunch, finally arriving in front of Bill, the real Transport Minister. I took him by the hand and leaned close, my mouth an inch from his disgusting misshapen ear. I whispered "Bill. You are a bastard". Though this joyous event only occurred in my head, forced to maintain the same dull demeanour as Bill. For a time I had suspected him of faking it, that he may have been moonlighting in similar fields as myself. Though a few nights of investigation found him to be just as boring as he appeared, that and a terrible lover with an unappetizing wife. So I simply shook the boring man's hand as images of his sweaty body humping his horse faced wife flooded through me; producing an appropriate mournful grin of a colleague's departure.

My driver was waiting outside for me. Holding the door open. He was privately employed. Odd that the Transport Minister would not be allowed a company car. My driver as his title suggests, drove me home. I entered into my fake apartment. At the bar I poured myself a scotch and sat down on my couch, spreading the documents before me. The contents rather droll. The exciting stuff would come significantly later. For now, in the first few months I would be actually doing my official job. Working hard at the boring stuff, until I could find another Bill. A hard working bore that I could burden with the bulk of my work. From the information in my hands a few candidates were beginning to reveal themselves. One woman by the name of Linda looked interesting. Overweight with an overbite and overbearing husband. She repulsed me. So I chose to focus on one of the more appealing creatures. A young woman called Jessica. Twenty-two with dirty blonde hair and a skinny neck. The strain of the tendons alluded to large breasts, her I.D. photo allowed only the slightest glimpse of cleavage. Forcing my imagination to fill in the gaps.

After a few moments of euphoric interlude I noticed the corner of the page flicker. A draft in the room. It could have meant a million things, though right at that moment I knew from where the current was coming. With the pistol in my right hand I crept toward the fireplace. Unlocked. I walked in. I raised the gun as I entered my bedroom. She barely reacted to the barrel pointed towards her face. I let it linger before placing it on the bedside table. Monica looked almost disappointed, she lifted the sheet to allow a glimpse of her firm small breasts. I took my clothes off myself. Undressing each other was not a pleasantry which we were accustomed to. As if to do so would be to acknowledge that some feeling of mutual admiration or adoration existed in the deep recesses of our hearts. No words were spoken, her mouth wet, her tongue twisting down my throat. It didn't last long, I had given up on prolonging the inevitable when it came to Monica a long time ago. Once upon I time I would think of any number of unsavoury events, ugly people, decapitations and malaria; all for her pleasure. That was before I realised that sex was more about power than pleasure for Monica.

About 30 minute's passed. She was smoking in my bed. It pissed me off because the ventilation in secret apartments isn't the best. I conceded to her. Speaking the first words;

"What do you know?"

She smiled. I didn't look at her but I could feel that malevolent grin protrude from her icy lips.

"More than you"

The icy grin now adapted into a cackle, so sinister a panda in some unknown paradise surely killed itself. After a few minutes she filled me in on some minor details regarding what I should expect of the next few weeks. She got up. Her body now sheathed by a black sheer dress that clung to her hips with alluring intent. The dress went well with her thick, shoulder length black hair, always worn up. She was a venomous snake, inhabiting a limitlessly tempting body. I tried exceedingly hard not glimpse her departure though I found myself wanting.

Alone I flipped through the pages of the documents before drifting to sleep.

The next day, my driver picked me up around 8 a.m. an ungodly hour in my opinion. I was keen to make a good impression. Though this impression would of course be a lie, most are. The trip was not very long. The Titan building was located only three blocks from the Epsilon building. My interview was on the fourteenth floor. Not much was said. I was rather disappointed that my interviewer was a minister of the same importance and pay grade that would accompany my future position. It was a telling sign that gaining trust in this company would be difficult. Though, my interviewer gave the impression that he was rather enchanted by my presence. I enjoyed the way his voice would raise a half an octave after every verbal blunder. Then he would smile and apologise. I felt empowered. Once the interview had concluded he shook my hand, his hand lingering a half second longer than standard procedure. He told me that he would be in touch in a few hours, and that I should keep my phone within reach. I told him that I would, that I was looking forward to his call, and finally that I wished to get lunch sometime in the near future. He winked. I shuddered internally at his repulsively childish response.

Having nothing to do for the remainder of the day I decided that it would be in my best interest to familiarise myself with what would soon be my workplace. The 17th floor was the transport department. Titan's department builds the cars themselves, while Epsilon builds trains and roads. It's an even split. I made sure my driver didn't work for either. He was a mangy bastard I picked up in the Jungle Prison seven years earlier. He never spoke and always looked as if he permanently had a bad taste in his mouth; he also happened to be a complete psychopath. A fact which was fine by me, it came in handy every now and then. I had never met an individual so contented to dispose of bodies. Contemplations about necrophilia and other such pleasant habits often crossed my mind, though, something about him seemed beyond the realm of sexuality. With all of that said, he would stack up to be the best of my employees.

Finding myself among what was soon to be my staff, a wave of deflation washed through me. All of them as boring and plain as the last. From the water station I spotted Jessica. She was not as captivating as I had hoped though I commended myself when I noticed the heaving of her chest. I thought at the time that perhaps we would become an item, an interesting approach to the situation, though she had four years of knowledge, all of which would give me some leg up in establishing myself in the company. Then I spotted Linda, her face was that of a small inbred dog, her body looked as if it was constructed from the goo which children play with, as a means of developing creativity. Whatever child constructed this monstrosity was sure to go on to do tremendously insidious things. I pondered how such a creature would come into existence. Thanks to the miracles of science this woman would have access to thousands of treatments to cure her disfigurement. Perhaps she had sought such treatment out. Perhaps things went poorly. Or maybe, Chancellor Jenny Reynolds promotes this behaviour, she herself a feminist, though of course her activism took a form inspired by Rand. Under this model it would seem that these surgeries were the moral course of action. I simply assumed from then on that she was some force of nature, whose imperfections could not be defeated. She would still make a good Bill, though I would need to find ways to limit our contact.

I phoned my driver. He picked me up outside. He killed the engine. He exited the car and opened the rear passenger door for me. It was a procedure we had established months earlier after a rather unsettling incident. It was late, or early depending who you asked, I had just exited the Sector 14 apartment of a Jungle crime boss. He would be found the next morning riddled with 9mm bullets, his severed hand clutching his shrivelled penis. It was an easy job and it had to be done. The gangs were planning to destroy the outer wall. Their plan to create and smuggle fertiliser explosives was of course idiotic and would never have succeeded. None the less the Infrastructure department would suffer some backlash. The way we handled things was cleaner. Or so I thought. I left the body, kept the gun. No one would be looking for it. I descended out into the night. Opened the door, my seatbelt locking into place. Then I realised the gun lingering at the side of my driver's head. The assailant was young. His hair an unfortunate shade of ginger. I would never know exactly what he was expecting from the situation. He opened his mouth. The gunshot overshadowing his demands. The boy's blood lapping in the front passenger seat. My driver pulled away from the curb. Neither of us spoke as we drove on through the night. Soon arriving at the Sector 27 scrapyard. We both got out and watched as the compactor crushed the car and its contents. We phoned Monica. She brought us back to the Inner City. I would awake the next morning to find an identical car sitting on the street below my apartment.

From that point on I would be perceived as just as pompous and stuck up as the rest, every time I made my driver open my door. Once we were both inside I asked him if he wished to engage in lunch. He declined. He always did, though I often asked simply for the fun of it. The routine. We drove home. My phone buzzed a kilometre from my doorstep. It was my interviewer, I would be starting tomorrow. I thanked him for his time and hung up. My driver dropped me 200 meters from my doorstep. The walk was short, I wasn't feeling particularly active. A large package of groceries placed at the foot of my door. The drones dropped them off twice a week. Full meals are more common and significantly cheaper, though I preferred to make my own cuisine. I despair at the inexplicable fried and processed muck, the blandness of vitamins. My earliest memories took place in the kitchen of our townhouse in Tetbury. The kitchen sat below the rest of the house, the sunlight shone down, igniting the room, only shadowed by the legs of occasional passers-by, walking down the street. My family shared what was once an 18th century Cotswold stone building, now split into eleven separate town houses. Remnants of the previous stained glass littered our end of the dwelling. Coloured light littered through the cracked panes. In this environment I learned the art of pastry. My mother's soft hands helping me mix and knead the dough. The platinum of her hair painted a soft orange by the light passing through a glass star shaped window. She would die the day of my twelfth birthday. My father would leave two days later. I would be left enfolded in the light and memories of a dead mother. The day I learnt that my father passed I baked a soufflé.

The package contained an assortment of meat, vegetables and a few items of fruit. I crafted a beef and mushroom pie. Eating it alone at my fake dining table, I found myself missing the simplicity of childhood. Nothing would ever be as sweet.

Chapter 12

My office was smaller than the last one. The light a little too bright, no doubt to stimulate the worker bees into productivity. It bothered me. My chair was also the kind that swivelled, that also bothered me. It had been four hours, I had already made two promotions. Jessica was now my personal assistant, her desk arranged outside my door, at an angle that allowed me to fixate my stare of wondrous imagination directly towards her ample bosom and would simply seem the natural progression of an absent minded gaze. The other benefactor of my keen eye for potential being Linda. She was significantly more excited than I had expected. She wrapped her monstrous warped arms around me. A dampness seeped through her. I reminded myself to dispose of the jacket later. Linda would now be the, *Junior Transport Minister*. In some months I would promote her to *Vice Minister*. I would have to wait. If the promotion came so soon Linda may have been actually recognised for her potential, I couldn't have that. It would have to be my vision; my foresight into the potential of this beast. Jessica would also become more effective, this however would not last. The entire office would pick up the pace regardless of my managing ability due to Hawthorne effects.

My first day was going rather acceptably fine. I had approved the production of four new rail designs. Three of these designs would be produced in Sector 15, from close to quality materials, then shipped and sold throughout The Union. The last design would be sold within London, the materials would be poor and the designs intentionally ineffective. Each designed so that every component would eventually expire and could then be easily and effectively replaced. The irony of this system was yet to dawn on me, at this time.

The day was coming to an end when my interviewer arrived in my office, standing awkwardly with his hands folded within one another, like a school child posing for their class portrait. His words were slow and deliberate though his gaze never stayed focused on anything particular;

"I was wondering, if you would like to come out tonight. Celebrate your first day, you know?"

He blushed a little.

A few others, including Jessica, accompanied us. The club was in Sector 8. A four storey building without windows. The bass rippled through the ground in a three kilometre radius. A line as long as fifty people littered the street. I was familiar with the establishment, on occasion I would dump a body or two in one of the restrooms. The bouncer had been on my payroll for quite some time. He saw me at the back of the line. For a brief moment he averted his gaze, fixating upon the curious cracks in the pavement. Quickly his attention returned to us, pretending that he just recognised me. He invited us to the front of the queue. With a smile and a tip the bouncer opened the door into the neon hellhole that people straight facedly call, 'nightlife' A hostess guided us towards a table. My interviewer offered to pay for the first round. I allowed it. My interviewer returned, though at this point he was no longer just my interviewer, he was Timothy; the HR Manager and near hairless, boy-man. Timothy placed a few pills and a bottle of scotch in front of me, Jessica was drinking martinis, she would pull a sour face with each gulp, there were many gulps. I spent the majority of the evening, admiring her attempts to sheath her disdain for the taste. She spent the remainder of our time talking at me. I would nod and smile, laugh when prompted by her own cackles. Luckily the blaring noise surrounding us protected me from any and all details that she was spouting. Every few minutes I would turn, my eyes tracking Timothy across the dance floor. The vigour and energy of his movements were astonishing. Cocaine and ecstasy really do make all the difference. Eventually Jessica pulled me closer to the crowd of sweaty, drugged up, dance-zombies. I spotted two of my employees cannibalising each other in the corner, if they were more attractive it wouldn't have been so disturbing. They weren't, and it was.

I was the only one, out of the three of us that remembered the trip back to Timothy's apartment. Also the only one to remember the ensuing intercourse. In truth, neither Timothy nor Jessica really engaged in the act of a threesome. It was more like sharing myself with both of them. The logistics a bit harder on account of Timothy's aversion to the breasted. Though all and all, I enjoyed myself. The morning after, almost as interesting. Light filtered through the windows, eventuating at the base of Jessica's exquisite chest. Timothy's arms extending past me, his fingers resting on her hips. It reminded me of mornings spent in my bed with mother, only I actually held something close to positive emotion for my mother. Timothy's apartment smelt like leather-bound books and treated wood. While they slept, I perused the spines of his novels. Half of them were prohibited. On the top shelf stood an amass of first and second edition novels, a second edition *Lolita,* a first edition *Anna Karenina,* in the original Russian. Positioned intentionally at the core of the arrangement, sat a second edition copy of *The Great Gatsby*. I stepped back, noticing all of the spines completely intact; the irony was literally palpable.

Timothy's tablet was left unattended on the breakfast table, it was locked though Timothy wasn't in a position to prevent me from scanning his thumb print. The contents at first glance were rather dull, everyone is cheating on one another. A couple of division mangers feel suicidal. Lastly a mine in Sector 30 was closing down and the senior staff were in the process of being moderated. It wasn't much but some of it would be useful. I committed the details to memory before dressing myself. My driver picked me up outside, I changed at home into a new suit before arriving at the office. It was still early, the cleaning drones my only company. I had given my driver my best estimation of Jessica's measurements. He would return soon with a pantsuit and some makeup items. Jessica would no doubt arrive, dishevelled and possibly still inebriated.

Various documents littered my desk, mostly cost/benefit analyses. I poured through a number of them. The premise itself so insidiously morose. I dumped more than half on Linda's desk, attaching a little note with a smiley face, I hoped this would make it easier to swallow, or much harder, I didn't particularly mind which. All I knew was, I hated dealing with cost/benefit analysis.

Over the course of the next few hours, my employees slowly poured in. Some hangover, most unhappy, all of them unfulfilled in their lives. Linda was the only one of the bunch who looked even close to pleased. The smile only slightly perturbed by the mountain of documents. She seemed like the work addict type, one of those disturbed creatures who actually gets off on stock projections and all that other crap. I guess when you look like a demented gingerbread-man, even maths can become sexual. I watched her as she sat down and delved into her fantasy. I ran through a couple of documents, signed something; no recollection of exactly what. The boredom had set in early. I found myself staring at the wall more often than usual. My driver eventually remerged. He found his way into my office, placing a coffee and a bacon sandwich on my desk, a clothing bag on the floor.

"Want to eat with me?"

"No, I already ate."

"Want to anyway?"

"No."

"Careful now, you might hurt my feelings."

My driver left me chuckling in my seat as he departed my office. A few of the worker bees acknowledged his presence, most averted their eyes. Jessica gathered significantly more attention when she stumbled into the office almost an hour late. Her makeup was smudged and it was clear that she had slept in her clothes. I signalled her to come into my office, she obliged. Neither of us exchanged more than a smile, kicking the bag towards her, she blushed, clearly somewhat embarrassed. She exited, off to find the nearest bathroom. That little interaction would no doubt be the highlight of the morning. Monotony plagued the rest. Linda eventually handed back all of the documents notarised and approved. I gave her the remainder of mine, along with a two hour lunch break. This left me with nothing at all to do. I considered getting a message to Monica, though it was possible that my communicator was being monitored. Best to wait until she next turned up in my bed. She would always some way or another find herself materialising around me, just to make sure I wasn't too fulfilled in my existence.

The sun was hiding itself and the view from the window obscured, as if nature itself was tormenting me with banality, even Jessica in her new clothes was beginning to bore me. It fit her well, though the cut was more conservative than I was accustomed to. I laughed at the thought of my driver attempting to spite me. It would seem possible when concerning any other organism, but not this one. He was the most straight faced bore I had ever met. Ridiculing him was one of the few joys in life that could always be counted on. If these taunts actually produced a response, the fun would either be increased or diminish significantly, I was unsure as to which. Though he was certainly good at his job, his lack of personality and chalkboard demeanour made things easier. I had once witnessed him break a man's leg with a tyre iron. At first I thought it a curios place to strike a man, though I soon learned; that a shattered femur will never grow back right. At this time, in my dark lonely office, I found myself missing that psycho.

I took my lunch break late in the afternoon. The building had a cafeteria, filled with fried foods, sugary treats and all the vitamins and dietary replacements you need to trick your body into thinking itself to be healthy. Once people would stick their fingers to the back of their throats in order to create room for more food; now we have pills to do the hard part. I would not be eating there. I walked a few blocks to a café that I had once frequented a few years back, during a slander campaign, digging up dirt on a journalist so high and mighty that he actually investigated things that mattered. I would watch his apartment from the café, in time he would reveal himself to be not only a frequent client of a particular dominatrix but also a staunch liberal. The raids uncovered over two hundred banned books and films in his collection as well as plans to create an underground newspaper and some connection to a fringe terrorist group. I still had his uncensored-bible siting in the draws next to my bed. I flipped through the pages every now and then. I can see how it worried The Union. Jesus, the great pacifist, allows himself to be crucified, for some reason God itself decides that slaughter is not the answer, as if Sodom and Gomorra were just the result of a bad day. Now what exactly could drive this literally perfect being to bear arms? Bankers. A whip, but still a weapon. The Union, however, kept the somewhat paradoxical part about the omnipotent being who for some reason needs three days to return to the earthly plane that it created. Though I suppose all that could be chalked up to symbolism and theatrics.

My branches into theology were cut short by the arrival of Jessica. She blushed as her eyes found mine. She was still wearing the pantsuit, though her hair was now washed, her nails painted yellow. She looked good. Patting the seat next to me she complied. Her smile was nervous and her lips were quivering slightly. I tried as best as I could to sound cordial, or playful.

"I don't remember giving you a second lunch break?"

"You didn't. I did."

The voice drifted from over my shoulder, the accent thick. Glasgow. She spoke with the confidence of age and the tone of someone who stumbled on to a conversational checkmate, a power play. I stood up from my seat and greeted the woman who would turn out to be Chancellor Reynolds. I shook her hand as she took the last of the empty seats. A waitress arrived at the table, taking with her the remnants of my lasagne. She would return in a few minutes with a pot of tea and six muffins, all different types, all insidiously small. In this time I had ascertained that Jennifer was Jessica's aunt. Jessica being more or less named after her. I struggled to comprehend the connection. Chancellor Reynolds had no known relatives according to Epsilon intelligence. Though, straight from the C.E.O's mouth.

"I wanted to thank you for what you did for my Jessica."

She placed a little too much emphasis upon the word 'did.' How much could the old lady know? I'm no prude but even I wouldn't embrace the opportunity to boast about my night of drugs, booze and blatantly weird sex. I decided to simply bow my head in modesty towards her apparent appreciation. Beyond that, there was little room for myself to interject into the conversation. The two simply would not shut up. Talk of work, food, social life and all the other various banalities one fills their precious time with before death. It would not have been such a bad experience if not for the fact that I actually had to pay some attention, this would be the start of my correspondence with C.E.O. One which would end rather upsettingly.

After several pots of tea, Jessica decided to depart, she had things to do before the work day ended. I cited the same reason for departing though the Chancellor denied me. Jessica embraced me before strutting back to the office, leaving me exceedingly perplexed.

"I do appreciate you promoting her."

She seemed genuine, something I was weary of when coming from business people. I tried to match her tone.

"She's a great girl, smart too."

"No, she isn't."

The old woman's word were spoken just as candid, with a slight shaking of her head as she continued.

"That girl's never been too bright. But she's personable. I, myself, could never promote her, can't have people think I'm one to play favourites"

Though of course she was always playing favourites, only she was always favourite, all others could hope for was second best.

"I was not aware that she was your niece, I would never do such a thing to gain favour."

"No. I assume you had other things in mind."

There was a pause, somewhere a whale beached itself.

"Perhaps."

With that, my last word the woman grinned and stood up from the table, I began to rise, though she signalled for me to sit down.

"You are doing good work for the company Mr Neals, that's all that matters to me."

With those words she departed, striding off towards the exit, her walk, that of a much younger woman. I devoured the last of the insidious muffins, wiping the crumbs from my suit pants, I messaged my driver on the way out.

Chapter 13

It was atrociously early on a Monday morning. Monica was blowing smoke rings in the air from under my sheets. It had been two months since her last visit. Sweat binding her legs to the white sheets. I had not intended to give into her. It wasn't that I had begun seeing Jessica, though I knew if I refused, she would conclude that I actually felt for another human being. She would try to hold that over or me, or perhaps use her against me. Together we pulled out a large sheet of paper, pinning it against the wall. Mapping out the various pieces of information, tapping files to the wall. Monica conducting the activity still unclothed. She gave a harrowing smirk each time she caught me focussing upon her nakedness. In honesty I believe she only wished to map it out this way as too show herself off, and maybe also demonstrate her penmanship. So few of our generation ever learnt to actually physically write. Nothing is tactile anymore.

So far all we had was the information about the Sector 30 mine that was in the process of closure, and the connection between Jessica and the Chancellor. Timothy would also be easy to blackmail if we needed any more information. The plan as it stood was to gain enough power and access to sink other departments in the company, Epsilon would then buy these departments out or perhaps muscle in on the market. There was nothing more that we could do at this time. Naturally, Monica filled the blank air with her unsightly words.

"Do you believe in God?"

My neck snapped instinctively towards her, my surprise amounting to her sheer delight.

"Why do you care?"

I stressed the sentence as long as possible as I tried to make sense of her. She ignored my question, replacing it for the one which she preferred.

"I believe in God."

"I suppose the Devil should believe in God."

She made sure not to laugh. Just starred with malevolence.

"We are doing God's work."

I was taken aback by her. On occasion she had seemed to be a poorly sheathed, self-serving monster of Gargantuan proportion, but never delusional.

"Most people don't aggrandise the wallets of fat, rich assholes to divine status."

"Epsilon will unify the nation and drag us out of debt, is it so wrong that some of us make a few credits along the way?"

She was baiting me, standing with her hands on her hips, a great imitation of the challenged offence she wished to convey. I refused to believe that she actually deluded herself into believing that we were in anyway the heroes. There are no heroes, in our story, there haven't been any heroes here for a long time.

"Then what exactly is God?"

Her reply was more honest then I had expected.

"God is power, God is control; the things that matter."

"Well I guess that's the convenience of God, he turns into whatever each arsehole wishes him to be, and naturally, a money grubbing harlot such as yourself would have no problem believing that God is a big believer in trickle-down economics"

"And what is God to you? A hypocritical, sex obsessed deviant?"

"Something like that."

She smiled, somehow I believed her joy to be genuine. She clothed herself and departed into the morning light. I waited a half hour before doing the same.

The office was already populated by the time of my arrival. By this point Linda had an office outside the door of which read; *Vice Transport Minister.* My office had also been renovated, adding a small bathroom with a shower, it was a nice touch. As I walked into my office Jessica handed me a large tea and a beef sandwich. Neither were my favourite though I had made an empty promise to 'try new things', it wasn't so bad, in exchange she agreed to cease dragging me to clubs.

I ate my breakfast at my desk, sitting firmly in my new carved wooden chair. It didn't sit right, my stomach was turning uncomfortably. It wasn't the food, something else was burning within me. Something I had never yet experienced. An ignorant observer would conclude guilt. Perhaps at the time I would have also believed the same, though that was never it.

The hours were passing as dull as always. Paperwork and shitty coffee. What occurred next could not be seen coming. Every day couriers arrived to the building, delivering highly classified documents. These couriers deliver to all major businesses. These files came directly from The Union, never in all our efforts has Epsilon been able to infiltrate the couriers. That's why when, all of a sudden six couriers that had never been seen before arrived in the building; no one questioned it. The men were all different in look, the one who could be considered the leader was clearly eastern European in appearance. All six of the men wearing the uniform typical of Union representatives, white overcoat and red ties. Four of the sub lings entered the separate offices of all major departments. I would not learn these details until hours later. A courier entered my office he placed the files on my desk.

"We have to talk."

He was a tall man with dark hair and sunken eyes. His words were stuttered and nervous. Proceeding to draw the inner blinds of the office. As he reached for the button I noticed that his coat drooped a little past the elbow.

It's not that I distrust the crippled, but I had a healthy suspicion of this man. I reached for the gun I kept in the third drawer of my desk, as I opened the file in front of me. The benefit of having all of your arms. The first page was blank except two words.

'We Know.'

The cripple was quick, but I was accurate. His shot pierced through my left deltoid muscle. The pain was excruciating though I popped a shot off before it could register. The bullet tunnelled through the man's right eye socket, fragments of his brain splattering against the blinds. There was little time to ponder the consequences of the man's forebrain painting the walls of my office, all the man's personality and memories caking into the carpet.

I pulled myself up, Jessica screamed as she ripped the door open, finding me peering over the man, his right arm amputated at the elbow. Jessica came forward to embrace me, though I pushed her and the others out of the way. Sending a warning to Epsilon on my communicator as I ran towards the Chancellor's office. The elevator was infuriating. They would get to the Chancellor last.

Heading out of the elevator, I saw the courier up ahead, thirty meters. He was close to *the Chancellor's* office, an office of people between us. I raised the gun and fired four shots, three of them would be found embedded in his chest, the last piercing his throat. Men and women alike screamed. A bulky man tackled me, everything went black.

When I awoke drones were hovering through the office, some armed. Jessica was holding me, my head resting in her lap. The bullet had been removed from me, the wound sown up while I was still unconscious. Powerful sedatives coursing through my blood. My blood that was still slowly seeping into the flooring. *Chancellor* Reynolds walked over to where I was lying. Her suit pristinely clean, solitary tears rolling down her face. I tried to sound like someone who hadn't been shot, though evidently I had.

"What's the damage?"

Her reply was in the broken words of a frightened woman, certainly distraught and confused.

"The other department heads are dead. A few others as well. Christopher in your department was also killed."

I had no idea who Christopher was, but I nodded my head in solemn mourning.

"They weren't from *The Union*, all the Chancellors are dead except for Epsilon's. There was also an attack on the Chairman. He survived."

"How did they get in? Why weren't they scanned? Who were they?"

She had begun to be frustrated with my questions. She spat her response back at me.

"Terrorists! They were scanned. *Union* people don't have tags, it appears these men all had their right arms surgically removed!"

The coats hiding their stubs.

The Chancellor began to walk away from me, towards a crowd of Titan owned policeman. She turned about seven meters away from me.

"Thank you Mr Neals, for saving my life."

With Jessica's help I limped back to the office. My employees had scattered. Probably already home in the arms of the people they paid to love. The man's body was still on the carpet, Jessica screamed when she saw the extent of the blood splatter. His pockets were empty though the file was still on my desk. I took the contents and spread them out on the floor, scanning each one in detail. I was losing blood and the adrenaline was slowly leaving my system, none of the documents resembling anything meaningful at the time.

My driver picked us up and dropped us home. I had tried to protest, I didn't want her there, and I would have much preferred to be alone. With Jessica there I would be unable to contact anyone at Epsilon. Though she flicked away my protests as if they were the simple products of bravery. I am many things, but I am not brave. She would learn that in time.

We entered the fake apartment, lay down on the fake bed. Though I had never intended, together we drifted off into the darkness. I dreamt of my schooldays, of bullies and boredom. One particular grunt named Benjamin, he was also eleven, though, big for his age. Benjamin vowed to make life hell for myself and all others that read at a higher level than he. Each day he would beat me and shove my face in the mud, kick me in the ribs while I was down. I hid it from mother as best as I could. She was in her final months and alarming her would only make things worse. Eventually I found ways to fight back. Once one of the cheap knives which used at home broke, the last few inches of the serrated blade snapping off. Mother asked me to dispose of the knife though I kept the blade. After school that day I let Benjamin knock me to the ground I shoved the blade through his pants into his calf muscle, the boy screamed and choked on his own voice. He collapsed beside me, shoving the rest of the blade in his mouth, I gave him three good cracks, before leaving him to scream at the dirt. My mother wasn't angry when they brought me home. She was only solemn. Solemn because she was beginning to realise what I was and that I would survive without her. My dream ended like most others, with her dying in my arms, collapsing onto the table as I blew out the last my candles, as if it were what remained of her life force. I awoke holding Jessica, my arms around her waist. Things were becoming highly unusual.

I suppose to an ignorant observer sharing such things would seem sentimental, mistakenly so. Dreams are little more than the uncontrollable aspect of our vicious, primitive imaginations. Memories are just subjective interpretation of subjectively memorable events. It is not due to weakness that I admit these things, sometimes our interpretations are important in creating a bigger, clearer view of the truth.

Jessica woke before me, she remained in my arms consciously for at least an hour. I found it to be rather unsettling. Her breathe was less fowl than I had expected. Breaking one of my long held rules was an unwelcomed occurrence.

"How'd you sleep?"

I was unsure how exactly to answer her question. Though somehow honesty seemed the appropriate response.

"As well as is expected with the amount of pain killers I had in me."

She smiled as she left the bed, moving to the kitchen, she opened a food basket left by a work colleague. The spread was mediocre, mostly processed pastries and various pills, indulging in only the few pieces of fruit in the basket. Both of our communicators buzzed, there was a meeting at the office in an hour to discuss who would be moving up in the ranks, who would be taking the dead men and woman's jobs. There had been no message from Epsilon or Monica.

Jessica helped me shower and dress myself, then together we proceeded to the office.

The halls were mostly empty, the building felt strange without the constant low drone of the gossiping worker bees. Instead there was just silence, sweet blissful silence. It would only last for a few hours.

The meeting comprised myself, a Union official, the head of the Titan police force, a few lawyers and of course the Chancellor, her assistants and advisors. The discussion began with the few details recovered about yesterday's events, the Chancellor read from a pre-written and no doubt heavily censored statement.

"We are under attack. We knew that there were people out there gunning for us. That's the price we pay for our position in this country. Wherever there are people willing to change the world, there are others who will only destroy. It appears that the group responsible for yesterdays is a terrorist cell calling itself *The Dissented Patriots*. Seven members infiltrated the building at 12:00 PM, five of the terrorists entered the offices of our five major department heads. Four of these ministers were killed, another six employees were also murdered. Mr Neals, the Transport Minister survived the ordeal and managed to eliminate two of the terrorists. The leader attempted to assassinate myself, Though Mr Neals shot the man before he arrived in my office. The last of the terrorists found her way into the server room. Her attempts to transfer any documents were unsuccessful, though she managed to escape. The police are currently attempting to track her."

Her voice was monotone throughout the briefing. One of the lawyers, a young pencil shaped man raised his hand before verbalising his question.

"Why were these people allowed in the building?"

The Chancellor cringed and clenched her grey teeth, before spitting out her response.

"The perpetrators were scanned for tags, though they were posing as *Union* officials, whom as you all know do not have tags! It turns out that these terrorists, these vile creatures had their arms severed in order to make it impossible to track them."

The lawyer didn't seem smart enough to register *The Chancellor's* frustrations with him.

"Could we perhaps learn their identities by looking through I.D tags that stopped transmitting?"

For some reason I felt the need to speak, perhaps cut the young lawyer down a few pegs.

"That's a long list. You realise the numbers of people that are murdered, disappear or die out in the Jungle?"

"Not to mention the Desert. We already checked city records, no unknown disappearances,"

She stretched the last word as she stared into the young man's soul.

The head of the Titan police force stood up from the table, he was a short balding man with a pencil moustache and chemical induced muscle tone.

"The terrorists left a series of files on the desks of the murdered department heads, contained within were miscellaneous documents, gibberish mostly. At this time we believe these files to be red herrings."

He sat down, the room was quite. I didn't believe him, though admittedly I was deducing out of ignorance, having yet looked at them. I was in desperate need to send them off to Epsilon, on the chance that they received different files or no files at all. I left my communicator at home on the chance that it may be proximity hacked. The young lawyer raised his arm. He perpetually whispered his question.

"Why? I'm sorry. Why? Do we know why they, um, did this?"

The short man turned to the Chancellor, she nodded. The short man nodded back.

"We believe this terrorist group may wish to undermine The Union."

The meeting took another shift in focus. One of the assistants pressed a button on her communicator, seconds later a short woman in a blue pantsuit entered the room, and she couldn't be more than five foot tall. A fringe cut into her hair, her makeup stained by perfect raindrop tears; she looked like a child. I recognised her from Timothy's HR records. Amy Laurence, She was the now the most senior of the human calculators in the finance department. Her boss and mistress was one of the spontaneous victims of the *Patriots*. Her voice was stuttered by grief, her composure compromised.

"*The Union,* has notified us that we must meet all of our production and domestic sales targets for the quarter, despite… recent events."

The room cringed, most because of the improbable goal in front of us, myself because of the ugliness of her failed attempt at stoicism. No one had any questions directed towards Amy, she was signalled to leave.

The eldest and greyest of the Chancellor's assistants rose from the table. He took the Chancellor's hand, it was a strange act of welcomed affection.

"In order to meet these targets; some changes will need to be made. Some of us will need to step up and take some extra responsibilities."

The man left an extended moment for his words to sink in.

"Ms Laurence outside, she will be stepping up and becoming the new head of the finance department, Mr Neals, he'll be stepping up and becoming acting head and supervisor of all major departments."

The grey haired man continued talking, though I stopped listening. Too focused on the implications and opportunities generated by my change in position. My mouth salivating at the promise of the various secrets and lies which would soon be in my hands. Though something close to panic was still lingering within the tissues of my stomach. After so many weeks of monotony and boorish paperwork, things were finally amounting to something. Granted, that it did take the deaths of multiple people.

The grey haired man stopped talking. People nodded silently, then proceeded to exit the office. One of the lawyers escorted me back to my office, a large stack of folders and tablets in his arms, I could have helped him carry the mountain of documents, though I chose not to. The office was extraordinarily clean, absent of all the blood and brain matter that had caked into the carpet and blinds, I would hypothesis that they had been removed and replaced during the night, though such an undertaking would seem implausible in such a small amount of time.

The office did look larger without the dead man on the carpet.

I organised the documents between departments, then sent for the senior members of those departments to help with deciphering the rhetoric and a general briefing of what the fuck was actually going on. If we were ever to strike, now would be the time.

I gave six hours of attention to the documents. Even if the attack didn't occur, Titan would still be behind. Their major mining industries were all having efficiency problems, machines had broken down, and several skilled engineers had been murdered. Titan's agriculture department was also slowly becoming crippled, a combination of parasites and the beginning of what would be a long drought was killing much of the crops. Intentionally sinking all of Titan's departments would allow Epsilon to swoop in and destroy whatever was left.

Chapter 14

Monica was wearing a black trench coat that only went down to her knees. The sight of her made me salivate a little. I wondered if male Black Widow Spiders lust after their female counterparts right up to the moment their heads get ripped from their abdomen. In days of youth the concepts of both hatred and sexuality alluded me. Now for years I had been dealing with both, wrapped up in a serpent of a woman.

We had decided to meet in a bar in Sector 18. It was dark and desolate, a perfect environment for talks of betrayal and terror. The City was a hotbed of cameras and surveillance technologies. Out in the Jungle, the threat was significantly decreased. Except for the justifiable panic set in by every dirty faced man, woman and child with sleeves covering their right arm. Monica was looking through the documents on my communicator, I had only just sorted through them myself. There was 50 pages in all. 47 of these pages appeared in code, stars, ampersands, old religious symbols. Fifty symbols to each line, twenty lines, no spaces. The order of the symbols was different in the Epsilon documents, the pages without symbols were the same. The first page read;

We Know

Cryptic and tediously vague. The second of the written pages expanded the theme, comprising a list of what they believed themselves to know:

We Know: about France.

We Know: about Greece.

We Know: about Italy.

We Know: about Spain.

We Know: about Switzerland

We Know: about The United States.

We Know: about Canada.

We Know: about Australia.

We Know: about Malaysia.

Perhaps the terrorists were demonstrating their geographical knowledge, though it seemed significantly more likely that these statements were references to the real fates of the listed countries. The Union has never, and will never address the fate of the other indebted countries, the hope is that one day the population will no longer remember the war, or the bombs or perhaps even the existence of the outside world. Rumours were intentionally spread throughout the populace about hypothetical bombs being dropped on hypothetical cities. Though the truth is way more sinister, chemicals rained down from the skies. Nations fell, literally fell; men, woman, children collapsing in the street. Future saints, adulterers, paedophiles, insomniacs, socialists, fiscal conservatives, classical musicians and even the all too rare appreciator of the banjo; all of them lying dead in the last places they drew breathe. France is now the favourite holiday destination for wealthy *Union* citizens, the Louvre's wings now desolate and empty. Australia is now, in half a uranium mine, the other half is a hole to dump waste in. The U.S's cities lay empty, crumbling as nature slowly begins to heal the deep and infinitely wide wounds by 'the Great Experiment,' a decrepit reminder of the costs and repercussions of first world dreams. Monica supported my hypothesis. Though between us we could not figure out exactly what the terrorists would gain from revealing their knowledge of this information.

The last page of the document was a printed photo, a beach, an Australian beach. Close to a thousand people littering the sand and the water. A red, oversized blimp floated overhead a banner read 'Celebrate 2070 with Lex!' 2070? It didn't make much sense.

Monica noted my confusion, I had been studying the details when she raised her maniacal lullaby of a voice.

"What's gotten you so bothered?"

"I thought, Australia was an energy farm."

She looked at me as if I were an adolescent she had just caught me, pants around the ankles, attempting to make passionate love to an inanimate object, such as a couch or a filing cabinet.

"The whole thing? How dumb are you?"

"The reports say..."

She cut me off with a laugh that was meant to mirror hysteria. Multiple bar patrons turned their attention to the beautiful sinister creature.

"You're smart enough to know that the majority of *Union* documents are largely B.S."

She put a little too much emphasis on the 'S'; attributed to the six drinks she had downed in the last hour and a half. Rarely had I witnessed her relinquish so much control.

"What's Lex?"

"It's a drug, a mood stabiliser. Basically an ecstasy infused antidepressant."

It sounded horrible.

"That sounds terrific."

Monica walked over to the bar and ordered herself a cocktail, I didn't ask her to buy me a drink, though one appeared in front of me. It was odd, being far too perplexed by the unnatural level of basic human decency which she was currently displaying.

"What should I be doing with my new position at Titan?"

I had already briefed her on the documents I now had access to.

"You ought to keep pushing paper. We'll brief you when it's necessary."

She spoke in the tone of a high school philosophy teacher, the drunken slurring adding to the impression.

"That isn't good enough Monica! I need information."

I didn't intend to blow up in her face, though the frustration rapidly dug its way to the surface. A silence drifted between us. I noted her expressions, doing the maths, deciding what information she was willing to give up.

"The Chancellor is putting the takeover in motion, some projects will be replicated, and others bought. Keep working, give us whatever relevant information you come across."

We both finished our drinks and entered separate cars

My driver had been waiting outside throughout the entirety of our conversation. He looked even more pissed off than usual as he held my door open. We didn't speak as we passed through Sectors. He declined to join me for a nightcap.

Chapter 15

Jessica arrived at my apartment early in the morning, she made pancakes and burnt coffee. We ate in my fake living room. She was wearing a dark maroon dress, enfolded in the dawn light she looked perplexingly beautiful. I would have told her, only soon I would never see her again. In some ways an attachment was blossoming between us, for her this attachment was littered with romantic undertones, she had begun to introduce me at dinner parties as her *significant other*, an insidious itch would present itself, mysteriously at the side of my neck. For myself the arrangement was a convenient act of stress relief with the added benefits of access to the very woman whose company I was determined to destroy. In previous evenings Chancellor Reynolds had invited us to spend dinner and drinks with her in her Sector 2 house. An 1890 Victorian, the structure previously stood in a town in North Somerset, now moved a block from Ludgate Hill, St Pauls Cathedral slowly crumbling, still an incomparably beautiful sight. The Thames clearly visible from the dining room. Private security littered the corridors, submachine guns in plain view. Nothing remotely interesting was discussed at dinner, due to the various straight jawed gunman which stood still and solitary in the corners of all rooms. Since the attack the Chancellor had become unnerved, she had developed the look and demeanour of a woman vacant of sleep, always on the verge of panic. Her fluffy white Pomeranians reflecting the same, she had begun to starve them, aggression flourishing within. They would yap and growl at most, though not I. The Chancellor attributed this mistakenly to my trustworthy nature, the dogs liked me because I had been feeding them foie gras and fish eggs under the table. After dinner we would have silent drinks in the lounge area, the dogs jumping on the lounge to be closer to me. Jessica would attempt to pat them, they would flash their lightning like fangs, forcing Jessica to recoil. She would get up and browse the book cabinets, feigning interest in the spines of the Chancellor's novels, she often came back to a specific copy of *The Fountainhead*, one of at least twenty copies. Sadly one orifice of conversation that never ceased to entertain the Chancellor was ethical philosophy, though never in the way most appreciators of thought would expect. Never any mention of Spinoza, Mills or even Kant. Just egoism and objectivism, as if morality is limited to what one can do for one's self.

"'To say "I love you" one must know first how to say the "I"', what an incredibly insightful woman."

"Quite."

It was all you really could say in response to her narrow minded insanity. She had made similar remarks on multiple occasions. On one particular evening, the chef had left the kitchen to inform us that his wife had gone into labour a day early and that he wished to leave early to be with her.

"No, you shall stay on as you were contracted, 'If any civilization is to survive, it is the morality of altruism that men have to reject.'"

"'Be kind, for everyone you meet is fighting a hard battle.'"

I spoke the words into my recently empty scotch glass. The Chancellor glared her small beady eyes at me.

"Who said that ludicrous, drooling drabble?"

"Plato."

The resulting silence was delectable.

"What year did you read Plato?"

Since that night I had bitten my tongue and nodded at whatever the ancient woman had to say.

Jessica complained about the last of the dinners as we entered the office.

"I can't believe how miserably lonely that woman is. She never invited me to her place before the attack. Now she won't let us go."

The office was loud and frantic when we arrived. The slaves working themselves to the bone. It was perplexing, the desperate situation had actually created productivity. Threaten someone's livelihood and maybe they'll lift their game a little.

My previous department had been emptied, the Transport Department now occupied the basement of the Titan building, and I was given seven more assistants, Linda now chief among them. She was working harder than ever, doing more than ever, yet she managed to maintain her ungodly figure. The others in comparison looked gaunt, the stress and the long hours burning through them. The toll placed on the factory workers was far more considerable, twelve reports littered my desk, and all of them concerning separate matters of work related deaths. Skulls crushed under overworked and faulty machinery, sleep deprived workers passing out onto various sharp, shiny and burning objects, exosuits braking down, causing joints to sprain and shatter. It was all a mess, and not just for the powerless, a supervisor in Sector 32 had his arms ripped from his body, the factory workers were all executed, whether they were involved or not; there was shades of Roman in that.

The task of reparations would be long and difficult. Few would remember what specific interventions I signed my name to. I wouldn't have been able to save Titan, even if I actually intended to. Everything was going down, though, only few were privileged to this information. I spent hours pondering the possible fallout that this information would bring. Perhaps 20% of the staff would kill themselves, maybe another 30% would fall under the boots of *The Union*. If Epsilon weren't taking me back I would surely be put to death for incompetence. It was a scary thought, mulling over the possible outcomes of Titan's fall. It would seem in Epsilon's best interest to protect me, after all, the grave digger knows where the bodies are buried.

An assistant organised a site visit for each of the locations. Sector 32 being the only location that captured my interest and more specifically my imagination. The photos which accompanied the files were highly graphic, though a forty minute journey revealed the bloodiest scene I was yet to encounter.

The factory was five square kilometres in area, one of the largest and most efficient of Titan's industries was manufactured in the plant, preassembled pieces of future buildings. Large *modeller machines* littered the wings of the vast factory, each a different size, the machines would print the various parts of buildings, using multiple materials. These segments would then be loaded into trucks and shipped to western European cities. The entire operation only required two hundred base level employees and another twenty trained engineers, always with one senior supervisor on deck. It appeared that the supervisor had disagreed with one of the engineers on a matter regarding how much the transport vehicles could carry, this argument reignited once the tray of a transport vehicle ruptured, the contents spilling out onto a 43 year old worker named Daryl. Daryl's lungs had been punctured and 90% of his bones shattered. At this point the supervisor had retired to the bathroom, most likely in order to spill out the contents of his stomach. The original engineer then organised and persuaded forty of the workers into an assault on the supervisor's office. Security drones incapacitated twenty-five of the workers, the drones were destroyed and the supervisor was beaten to death over the course of forty minutes. Security forces arrived, though the workers had managed to secure the building using the printers and transport vehicles. Many workers fled during the raid, though they were all eventually slain. Walking from place to place, one was continuously reminded of the massacre, caked blood painted the floor and walls, all connecting and oozing into one another to create one vast pool of blood, as if a great beast was slain and removed from the factory. I walked the length of the factory several times. Blood pooled in the wrinkles of my leather shoes, they would stain and I would need to throw them away a day later.

As I inspected one of the now destroyed printers, I noticed a pain in the sole of my foot, the pain of a rocks at the bridge, though as I dug into the partially dry blood, bullet casings revealed themselves. With a handkerchief I cleaned the small, medium and larger pieces of metal. Most of the shots came from 45.mm assault rifles though some hand gun cartridges could also be found. I turned them over in my hand, the markings and symbols were foreign to me, though each was decorated with an engraved medical cross. I walked into the swallowing shadow of one of the larger printers, exiting a round from my own pistol, a 9mm; the Epsilon logo clearly visible on the side of the casing. The bullets would be of the same calibre, used for the same handguns. *The Union's* use of outside armaments perplexed me. It would seem counterintuitive to buy ammunition from foreign nations when an armaments factory is in your possession. I tossed the casings back into the blood and moved to where my colleagues were assembled.

"Union, says replacements for the printers won't come for another month, the replacements and revenue loss will have to come out of our end."

The Titan supervisor, stuttered and spluttered his way through the statement, eternally conscious that the many litres of his blood could have been spreading through the great puddle if the incident occurred under his watch.

"Well I guess no one is taking a bonus this year."

I tried to wain enthusiastic humour, we all laughed, all of us conscious that we were fucked. My driver dropped me back to the Titan building. I entered *The Chancellor's office*, she was barely awake.

"So… What do we do?"

Her use of 'we,' made my skin crawl, though she looked as defeated as one could possibly become, the quarter was almost up. She would lose it all, now it was just a case of finding others to drag into the abyss.

I dropped my report on her desk before replying.

"It's a mess."

She agreed.

"Literally."

"Keeping the factory will most certainly make it impossible to meet our quarterly target."

"Then, what do we do?"

She half reached to take my hand before regaining something close to dignity.

"Sell. Find a buyer and sell, as fast as you can."

She groaned and banged her head against the desk, I exited the building, sending a message to Monica on my way home, containing all the files.

"MAKE AN OFFER."

Her reply was ungodly swift.

"OFFER MADE. THE GAME BEGINS."

My driver dropped me off a block from my apartment, I starred at my ragged stained shoes as I walked through the cold. A few solitary droplets created an interesting patterns throughout the discoloured leather. Perhaps, it was my preoccupation with the sorry state of my footwear that kept me from becoming aware of the photo taped to the inner side of my fake apartment's door. It fluttered to the ground as I entered the apartment. My mushroom risotto was already finished and partially digested by the time I noticed the A5 piece of laminated paper, solitary on the tiled floor.

Confusion and panic rifled through my joints as I lifted the small picture. The photo depicted a man and his too fat son, smiling, the Grand Canyon displayed prominently in the background, the words 'We Know,' written in red text across the base of the photograph. That man and his son would now likely be lying dead in the newer greater canyon of the U.S. This thought was quickly expelled from the folds of my consciousness, replaced by fears for my own safety, fears that would not be easily extinguished. Sleep would become a difficult task that evening, even in the security of my real apartment. My hand hovering over the gun I now kept under my pillow. At 7am I was awoken by a solitary beep from my communicator, it startled me and audible yelp drifted out my lungs. The message read:

'PARASITE TODAY. VACCINE TOMORROW.'

I showered, dressed, ate and descended into the streets, ever conscious of the pistol tucked into my vest holster. My stomach sunken unusually so. My driver passed the chip to me in the car, neither of us spoke not that, this was unusual. We were both aware of what was going to happen, though the risk seemed much higher for myself.

Jessica was sitting at her desk, her face pressed against the hard surface. I pretended I didn't notice as I entered my office. The entire building was filled with moody and despairing faces, the news had apparently spread. Many would not escape the downfall of the company. I myself would be in some way an arbiter of their fates, picking and choosing which managers to keep, which to give up. Then I would take my leave, forever. To sit and drink, to read and whore my way through the rest of the debt years.

I opened the blinds as to observe the despairing crew. Only two in the office continued despite their impending doom, a young intern named Declan and Linda; ugly as ever. At least she brought some consistency to my life. If it were a perfect world she wouldn't exist, if it was a close to perfect world I would do everything in my power to ensure that she be put in line for senior Epsilon management as soon as possible, but it isn't, and I wouldn't. I would ensure she keeps a job, though sadly in this world hard work and honesty count for very little.

Jessica observing my open blinds entered my office. She was wearing a bright red dress, no makeup, her hair in slight disarray.

"What is going on? No one will tell me!"

I gestured for her to move closer, taking her hands and sitting her on my lap, my arms enfolded around her velvety torso.

"Everything is going to be fine for us."

And at the time I believed that statement to be true.

She moved to sit on my desk, her beautiful eyes meeting with my own, we would sit there for over an hour; that being all I could do to reassure her.

There was less than an hour until the end of the work day, Jessica had already left and would be waiting for me at my apartment once I was done. My driver would walk her through the door and wait outside until I arrived. I half wished I had asked for him to stay inside with her, not for her safety but the sheer displeasure which both would be subjected to.

After my very last lunch break, I walked towards the records room. A guard opened the door for me, the room was about forty square meters, the mainframes lining the left wall. Since the attack an employee had been placed in the record room, I showed him my I.D. and requested a file I knew had already been destroyed, as the little bald man thumbed through various filling cabinets, I walked to the mainframe and placed the chip in. I turned back, told the bald man not to worry as I exited the room. It was an odd anti-climax. As I was walking back towards my office all traces of my existence were being wiped from the Titan servers.

I exited the building, tossed the photograph of Elizabeth Taylor into a bin, and entered the car. Jessica inside, more beautiful than this morning, clean hair, with a perturbed smile, likely attributed to the time spent with my driver. We drove to a nice restaurant, ate in silence, drove home and made love for the last time.

Chapter 16

I awoke to a beautiful face, though not the one I had gone to bed with. Monica's demonic expressions glaring into the depths of my soul. I failed to conceal my dreaded surprise.

"Where the fuck is Jessica?"

Her response was sinister laughter, a rainbow somewhere erupted into a destructive tornado. She pulled back the sheet to reveal our nakedness. I tried to remain fixated upon her eyes as I again asked the question again, perhaps more measured.

"What did you do with Jessica?"

Monica smiled as if she was moving in for the checkmate.

"Nothing, she left hours ago. Don't worry, I wouldn't touch your little girlfriend."

I knew denying the accusation would see it to be true in Monica's twisted imagination, though I did it nonetheless, perhaps to prove it to myself.

"I was using her for information, it's done now."

"No it isn't."

I starred at her for some time, unable to process exactly what she meant.

"Reynolds knows your name, she knows your background. She needs to be eliminated."

I took a moment to process her logic.

"Why do I have to do it?"

"Because it cannot look like a murder.'"

"I'm sure you could find a way."

Monica glared at me, her fangs barely visible, though the viscous intent was unmistakable. Her acid streamed through her tone of voice.

"We could, but time would be wasted, and a lot more people will die."

I swallowed hard and agreed to her terms. Monica mapped out the details of the plan. I would arrive at the Chancellor's home later in the day bearing an olive branch from Epsilon, sign everything over and your name stays on the door, Co-Chancellor, etcetera, but never any real power. It wouldn't really matter if she accepted it or not.

I packed a bag with a clean jacket, some bribe money, a few tools and a 9mm pistol. I placed my dart gun into my vest holster, and exited out the door.

In the car I asked my driver if he wanted to have breakfast with me, he declined. Though of course this was expected. As I sat in the corners of a dark café in Sector 3 drinking strong cups of bitter coffee, I wondered what exactly would become of my driver once this was all over. It seemed unlikely that either of us would be asked to repurpose back into the company, even more unlikely was the idea that the driver would cease to be the driver. His capacity for violence and monotone psychotic behaviour would be ill-suited anywhere else. Some part of me pictured him walking off towards the sunset, towards the Desert, shotgun and butcher knife in hand. I wondered whether I would miss him, he certainly wouldn't be missing me. I wondered if contact between Jessica and I would continue, it seemed unlikely, though the possibility did not entirely repulse me.

As we drove into Sector 2 I reached into the bag, counting out a few thousand credits, preparing to pay off the guard booth. To my surprise the gate was already open, the guard's uniforms labelled 'Epsilon Security.' I laughed with intense relief. The logistics of bribes always killed me, so many pairs of dirty hands, separately those hands had no power but together, those hands become threatening.

As I approached, I noticed that, The Chancellor's lawn was slightly over grown, I thought perhaps the gardener was sick and The Chancellor had grown to learn compassion. It seemed unlikely.

To my surprise the door was unlocked and the halls empty, almost all of the lights had been switched off. I waited for half a minute before continuing throughout the house, I drew the 9mm, removed my holster and placed the coat over the gun. The kitchen, dining room, office and bathrooms were empty. The bedroom seemed the last viable option. I placed my free hand on the brass doorknob, stepping through into the large white bedroom, revealing The Chancellor, asleep in the middle of a perfectly made bed. Her body rigid and skeletal. I closed the door and grabbed a sedative from my bag, searching only took a few minutes, though once I returned my focus to the women she was sitting upright, her small black eyes glaring knowingly.

"I've been waiting for you."

Her words croaked out as you would expect from a mummified body. I continued towards her the gun now clearly viewed in my right hand, the syringe in my left, tucked under, ready to strike. She continued.

"I'm not what you think I am!"

"I doubt many people believe themselves to be as deplorable as 'I think they are.'"

She was not amused, tears streamed down the ancient caves and valleys of her face.

"The *Union* isn't real! The debt isn't real!"

I laughed a little, amused by what I believed to be spontaneous creativity. I moved towards the bed and sat down on the edge.

"Open the bedside table, I have proof."

I flushed the 9mm into the side of her skull, I imagined it would cave in if I doubled the amount of pressure.

"You open it."

The Chancellor reached past me and opened the drawer. A great manila envelope weighing in my hand. I moved down the bed, placed the syringe within reach and tore open the great package. Over a hundred documents spilled out, some hard drives as well. Still holding up the pistol while perusing some of the documents. Much of the details had been redacted, the files regarding various exports to nations that had been supposedly destroyed. One particular photo stood out, a Tower flying the American flag, made out of Titan building materials.

I had been studying the details of the photograph for about a minute pausing every few seconds to remind The Chancellor that my attention still remained with her. Up until we were both distracted by the sound of weighty footsteps, weighty footsteps which concluded in the driver producing himself out of the darkness of the corridor, a hefty revolver in hand.

"What's taking so long?"

With the deliverance of those words, The Chancellor attempted to take advantage, reaching for the syringe, without the necessary time to strike. I fired two shots into her chest. She deflated with a barely audible groan.

For quite some time, silence drifted between myself and the driver.

"What's that?"

He asked with emotionless curiosity.

"It's nothing."

For the first time since I had known the man he displayed something close to disappointment. Any other entity I wouldn't have questioned it, though, the driver was a different kind of beast. We raised our guns at roughly the same time, both pointed at the others frontal lobe, less than a metre between our muzzles, it was three seconds, or five eternities before they flashed. My gun went off before his, squeezing twice in rapid succession on the hairline trigger, the bullets burst through his skull. He fired a shot a milliseconds later, a last instinctive impulse fired as his brain shut down. The bullet landed far from the target, nicking the base of my neck. His body crumpled to the floor inaudibly, sharp pain splitting through my head causing me to fall back onto the bed. I lay there for half a minute before the adrenaline set in, taking my neck tie and wrapping it across the wound, I got up, placed the file in the bag and dragged myself into the car. No one stopped me as I sped my way out of the City. Blood poured slowly out of the wound, my vision blurry. There was no real plan, nothing I could do to survive; they would always find me. I got past Sector 25 before passing out at the wheel.

Piercing light ripped through the cracks in a blind, the light pulsating toward my eyes. My mouth tasted of metal, various tubes placed in my arms, nose and mouth. My neck no longer hurt, though the pain had spread everywhere else. I attempted to move my hands over towards the tube only to find that my arms and legs had been chained to the ground, a thin mattress protecting my spine from the hard concrete. I attempted to scream though the tube made it impossible, gaggle sounds drifted vacantly through the sunlit room.

It was near an hour before someone came to check on me. A young blonde girl with a half inch scar under her left eye, it was odd but it somehow added to her beauty. She checked the numbers on a machine positioned in the corner of the room. Satisfied, she flipped out a notebook and scribbled something before beginning to leave. Knowing I couldn't stand to stay still, I decided to speak up. Screaming as loud as I could. Her eyes met with mine, a smirk appeared across her face.

She mimed the words.

"Welcome back."

She sat down next to me and wrapped her hands around the feeding tube, yanking it out from surprisingly deep within. Vomit spewed powerfully, not too dissimilar to the world's worst fountain. She appeared to be expecting this because she stepped back a few paces to shield her from the splash.

She moved to free my arms and legs. I pretended to pass out before she untied my right arm. As she untied the knot and began moving to my other arm I grabbed her by the collar and with whatever strength left, pulled her down upon me, wrapping and reinforcing my forearm around her neck. She lost consciousness within ten seconds. Taking the key I unlocked the chain on the other arm and ripped out whatever tubes remained in me after my violent outburst, various fluids spurted across the room. Light headed I searched a rusted set of drawers in the corner of the room. A scalpel the only item of real use. The woman on the floor groaned as she regained consciousness. Lifting her to her feet, holding the scalpel to her jugular, I dragged her out of the room into the piercing midday light.

After the blindness faded and my vision returned, I came to realise the four handguns aimed at my face. Each of the gunman without their right arms. The woman in my own grip, the only one without a handicap.

"We need him, don't shoot!"

The little woman screamed the words in an apparent French accent.

"Need me for what, exactly?"

I replied, in response to what wasn't a question.

The gunman moved uncomfortably, waving the weighty pistols in my face. Our standoff lasted about ten seconds. I weighed up the options and realised that in my state I wouldn't be able to escape the guns of the four, or the guns of any others that would surely arrive after these men were disposed of. I let go of the woman and stepped back a few paces. She gasped as she collapsed to the floor, quickly recuperating she bounced to her feet and punched me powerfully across my face. I spat the blood out. It sat in the dirt at my feet.

"How do you feel about second impressions?"

The cell which they put me in was larger than I had expected. I was told, Union officials had once resided in these cages for a few days before they were 'replaced.' I had been left in the dark, both figuratively and literally, three times in the first evening I accidently walked into my water bucket, the last of the incidents causing it to spill all over the dirty floor, creating my own personal bog, it was a regular summer getaway. Adding to my overall discomfort was the pestering thoughts, the troublesome questions which proceeded to plague my imagination all throughout the evening. How could it be possible that the Union didn't exist?

As sleep claimed me, my thoughts drifted to evenings of prepubescent bliss, watching the news with my parents, hand in hand. This of course is before they hated each other, or before they knew they hated each other, or perhaps before I knew that they knew they hated each other. We had just finished dinner and were watching a television program which explored the history of artificial intelligence research. The program began with figures such as Turing, Colby and Stephen Hawking then moved on to others such as Elon Musk, the program was an hour in, just touching on the A.I. research ban of 2020, when the news suddenly cut in, announcing the formation of The Union. I can remember the looks of terror on my parent's faces. It wasn't long after, that the crockery began breaking on a regular basis.

Even after I awoke from the dream, the thoughts persisted. I recalled life as a young orphan, living in an all-boys school. Less than two years after The Union formed, all travel outside the U.K and Ireland was prohibited. Stories of men and women who left anyway often plagued the news, occasionally they would be found dead or incarcerated. The internet was ablaze with chatter and reports of The Union's iron fist. For almost a decade life in Britain came with a certain amount of terror, the endless calendar, with each day possibly the last. Then finally the Union took over everything. Monuments, libraries and cathedrals were destroyed as the Union began shaping the land in their image. It was not long after the takeover that I began my employ at Epsilon. Now I found myself aching in the dark, waiting for the dawn sky, wondering why I still possessed my left arm.

It would have been roughly 9:00am when the man arrived outside my cell. Every step he took down the stairs echoed repeatedly, giving me time to expect him. I stood straight with my hands at my sides. He wore a maroon army style getup with a yellow sash across his right arm, which, as expected had been amputated below the elbow. What made this man different was the biomechanical replacement arm which fitted into place where the other had been taken. The new arm was a few shades lighter than the man's own dark brown skin, the forearm of the mechanical arm was also insufficient in size, making the man appear severely asymmetrical. He pulled a crate over from the wall and sat on it a metre from my dwelling. A cigarette behind his scarred ears, the man began to speak.

"Good morning, Mr Neals. How are you feeling today?"

"I never knew a French woman to hit so hard, but maybe that's because I never knew a French woman before now."

The man chuckled as he took the cigarette, placed it in his mouth and lit it.

"Albertine is quite the extraordinary woman."

"Albertine, are you serious? What's your name? Aramis?"

He again chuckled.

"Duncan, actually. Enough pleasantries. Now, Mr Neals, let's get down to business. Do you know why we have decided to 'shelter' you?"

I searched for a snarky comeback, though whatever piercing words I was searching for eluded me. He continued.

"You are one special person Mr Neals. You're in excellent shape, mentally sharp, and how old are you exactly? "

"Thirty-six."

"Right, and in the past nine years you've killed almost forty men."

"Is that supposed to make me feel what? Shame?"

"Embarrassment, seems more appropriate."

I was far from sure of what exactly he was insinuating though he did not leave me hanging for very long.

"All those years a puppet. How much did you know about those men? Why did they have to die?"

Thought wasn't necessary, my answer had lurked in the folds of my consciousness for years before the question was asked.

"Greed."

He was surprised by either my honesty or self-knowledge. His eyes looking up as he lit another cigarette, retrieved from the recess behind his ear.

"Yes, but you weren't the only one."

The statement seemed as if it were designed to instil shock within me.

"Of course there were others, I'm sure all companies had a position for someone like me."

"You misunderstand, Mr Neals. You weren't the only Minister of Offense at Epsilon. Titan may have been the biggest competition, but there were many others. Now there is only one company left. Epsilon Incorporated."

"And *the Union?*"

"They never really existed."

With those words, Duncan stood up and moved towards the staircase. Leaving me in the unventilated room. It would be three hours until I would have any more company. I spent that time sitting cross legged on the floor attempting to figure out if and how I had been manipulated for so many years.

Duncan returned, Albertine and another military garbed soldier trailed behind. Unlocking my cage. The soldier's gun trained at my head as Duncan applied handcuffs and a blindfold and forced me up the stairs.

"Too bad, these pretty bracelets want look good on me."

I spoke the words to the shadow of the soldier. Duncan began to laugh.

"That doesn't even make sense, interjected Albertine!"

Eventually we arrived in a dark room, the vague hum of machinery and the dull light of monitors seeped through the blindfold painfully.

Albertine removed the hood, it was the first time that I actually got a good view of her. Green eyes, bright teeth, long legs. She looked unhappy, I wondered if she was lonely.

"Welcome to the revolution Mr Neals."

Close to seventy men and woman sat scattered throughout the dark hall. Albertine and I the only ones without an obvious handicap. Twenty or more of the men dressed in military garb, robotic arms gripping bulky assault rifles. Duncan stepped up to a makeshift podium assembled out of transportation crates. His voice boomed throughout the hall.

"Today my brothers and sisters, today our revolution truly begins. Our enemy are bigger than we are, and they know we exist. They know that we are coming for them, and they are scared. With the information in our possession we stand a chance. Together we will rise from the ash and dirt, we will spread the truth and support will come, from within or from the outside. Our suffering will not go untold for long. We will rise!"

The crowd stirred, there arms in a salute.

"We will rise!"

The sea of people slowly flooded out of the hall until it was only Duncan, Albertine and an anonymous transcript writer who sat in the corner.

Albertine shrieked.

"Why is he still alive?"

"He may be useful down the road."

After answering her Duncan turned his gaze towards me.

"I think it would be best if you sat yourself down."

The typist occupied the only chair so I lowered myself to the floor.

"Take this."

Duncan passed a large cup of water deliberately to my right hand. I sipped a little, trying to hide my immense thirst.

"You have a gift that none of us have, Mr Neals."

The typist's keys clicked and clapped noisily in the corner. I sipped deeper from the cup.

"When we picked you out of that wreck you were a mess. Before we could get you to a secure location and fix you up, certain procedures seemed…necessary. In the process of completing these procedures they were found to be unnecessary."

He let the words linger, knowing them to be intentionally troubling. I continued to sip the cup of water, trying not to focus too much on the dirty floor.

"You're saying there is a reason that I am still in possession of my dearest arm?"

"Yes and it's not so you can jerk off!"

Interjected Albertine.

Duncan moved his stare toward her, he appeared deeply amused. The keys clapped.

"No. When our agents found you, they themselves had no idea of your value, they attempted to scan for your identification, though they found that your chip had been deactivated."

He paused for a moment as to gauge my reaction, I failed to fully sheathe my puzzlement. He continued.

"As far as we can tell, only high up government officials can deactivate these chips. Do you know why someone would do such a thing?"

I was unsure and for some reason I gave them my best guess.

"Because they were going to kill me anyway?"

Albertine wasn't satisfied by that answer.

"Shut up, tell us the truth! Why are you here?"

Her anger pleased me, though I was frustrated that I would not be able to answer the question even if I wanted to. The keys clapped.

"How likely would it be that the government would send their best assassin in a bloody mess to a random Jungle town in the hopes that we would take pity on him?"

"It's not like they don't have enough money for dozens of fucked up plans."

Duncan laughed again.

"And what of the documents we found with him, all of it confirms the government's treachery."

Now Albertine began to address me individually.

"Who gave you the documents? How much did you read?"

No strategic response came to mind right away, honesty was an option though in my experience, honesty rarely ends well. Silence and a defiant stare my only options.

"Who shot you?"

Duncan asked the question, Albertine gave him a look of absolute frustration as she threw up her arms and walked away from us.

"A friend, or more like a work associate shot me."

"Why?"

The keys continued to click, reminding me that I couldn't avoid their questions forever, torture or boredom would cast the words from my lips eventually.

"He shot me because they didn't need me anymore, I killed Chancellor Reynolds for them."

"Reynolds gave you the package?"

Albertine asked, half turned around as her interest had once again spiked.

"Yes, it was a bargaining chip so that I would let her live."

"And you reneged on your end of the deal?"

I shrugged, there wasn't really anything that I could say. Duncan then asked the next question.

"And your friend, what happened to him?"

"He's dead now."

They both stepped away from me a pace. Perhaps remembering or realising what I was capable of. It took Duncan a few moments to recover and continue his questioning.

"Harry?"

"Yes."

"You didn't read the documents, did you?"

The keys rested for a moment. I couldn't bluff my way out of it.

"I didn't exactly have time. I would appreciate the chance though? Also why is she here?"

Pointing toward the anomalous woman in the shadows. Duncan laughed at my request, his broad smile taunting me.

"We are taking you to a different room, you will find a dossier of all the documents we have cleared for you to read. You will also find clothes and food. She is here to ensure transparency within our organisation."

"And do I get a copy of this conversation?"

Duncan smiled.

"Do you really want it?"

I looked at the typist in the corner of the room, her eyes barely visible, and her fingers still but ready to fire off my response.

"Click-click."

The room was small but brightly lit, with nothing more than an old wooden desk and a small bed with heavy metal springs. It was not entirely comfortable though in comparison to the previous night it was the height of luxury. The food I was promised consisted of stale bread, carrots and some raw milk. The hopes of a cow lurking around excited me. Perhaps I would be able to slaughter it and make a proper meal.

I forced myself to eat and left time to digest and attempt to keep it down before I opened the folder. Only three documents lay ahead of me. The first seemed to be an excerpt from a speech given in 2073 to the United States House of Representatives, by a politician named Nathan York.

'Esteemed members of Congress. I come before you today to bring forth what I and many others consider to be a pressing and troublesome issue, the People's Republic of the Kingdoms, continues to oppress and destroy its own people. The state formerly known as The United Kingdom, now enslaves its citizens. Internet access, a basic right has been effectively cut off, freedom in any sense has been ripped from this once great nation's citizens, and their populace are lied to and subjected to a never ending barge of propaganda. After The War, the UK was near bankrupt, the streets of their cities torn and cracked, out of thus rubble a devious and divisive regime rose to power, a government of greed. What did we do to stop this regime?

(Pause.)

Some of you may be thinking we gave aid. Some may think we continue to give aid, and this is true, but only if one defines aid as the exploitation of the suffering of others, our aid to this nation involves buying cars, pharmaceuticals and whatever else and then selling these products for a premium. In doing so we are aiding and supporting a monstrous and malevolent dictatorship. A dictatorship lead by a man whose name we do not know. In the past five years, the man known only as "The Chairman" has lied to and murdered his own people. They are united against an enemy that does not exist. Blinded to the outside world, and we, we make this nightmare a reality by supporting such a state.

I am not asking that we go to war. I am simply asking you to stop feeding the snakes.'

A footnote hung ominously at the bottom of the page. It simply stated that York's bill was voted down in the senate seven times, never to pass through.

The second of the documents was a photograph of a short bald man with pale skin and little hair shaking hands with the Chairman. It's surprising how many years of history were shaped by old bald, white males with unquenchable appetites. The caption told me that the other man was the President of Australia, the photo being the only image of the Chairman in a foreign nation.

The last document appeared distinctly different from the rest, it consisted of a brief summary of Duncan's plan for the following evening I was asked to absorb the details in preparation.

Chapter 17

I slept far better than I expected. Immensely surprised by the bowl of porridge sitting at the table inside the locked room. The spoon had sunk into the vomit like mixture, I gagged a little as I retrieved it. I chose to eat as fast as possible so the burning sensation would mask the awful taste. As soon as I placed the bowl back onto the table. I knew they were watching, I just didn't know how closely.

Walking to the door, some sense of nerves bubbled to the surface. The door handle was cool, I opened it leading to an empty blank corridor. Lights flickered revealing the lines of dirt and mould on the off white painted walls. There were no other rooms or hallways attached, just one door at each end. I was halfway through when a speaker in the ceiling activated, I recognised the voice, and it was that of Albertine.

"Good morning Mr Neals, I trust you managed to grind your way through todays... schedule. In a few seconds a uniform will drop into the room, you are instructed to wear every item, do not bother returning to your room, we will be watching anyway."

A package dropped out of a shutter in the ceiling. I undressed on the spot, sitting in protest would do nothing but slow down the process. The uniform involved dark cargo pants and heavy boots with a black jacket, a red Epsilon logo displayed prominently across the left breast. An I.D with my face on it was attached to a belt, my new name; *Jack Burroughs,* I laughed a little. The last item was a weighty digital watch, I strapped it to my wrist before proceeding into the next room, a vast metal garage. Albertine stood meters from the opening, her hands firmly glued to her hips and what seemed like a permanent look of dissatisfaction.

"Are you ready Jack?"

"Do I really have a choice?"

"Well that watch you've got on is loaded with explosives, you do have a choice; but one of those choices probably isn't a good one."

"You do see the irony in this?"

"Of course, where do you think I got the idea?"

Duncan walked over to us. A young man with long black hair following a few paces behind. His arms were both in order. He seemed uncomfortable without the eyeliner I assumed he spent most of life touching up.

"Is he French too?"

"Ukrainian."

The man replied.

"Oh, did that become a thing again?"

Duncan snickered

"Sort of."

A white panelled van pulled up. The driver was about forty years old, his arm had been amputated at the shoulder, his replacement arm looked much nicer and more ergonomic than that of the soldiers, Albertine and the Ukrainian were both wearing similar uniforms, though those bore Union logos, the only other addition being a gun belt on their hips. Before we entered the van, Albertine placed a bag over my head, then we proceeded to our destination.

After about 20 minutes Albertine removed the bag, revealing the deeply disappointing view of the Dessert, overgrown wildlife, decrepit buildings slowly sinking into the earth.

"What sector is this?"

"43."

Albertine's replied, filled with disinterest.

"Are we there yet?"

She glared at me with such intensity that I almost began to miss Monica.

The remainder of the journey took almost three hours, every half hour or so Albertine would reapply the bag as we entered what I assumed to be tunnels. WE were meant to arrive an hour earlier though unforeseen circumstances, which no one would inform me of, got in the way. The plan would have to wait for tomorrow. We arrived at Sector 12 as the sun was setting. The sector looked like an ugly imitation of the City, walking towards the hotel I couldn't help but feel unsettled. A feeling that would not ease.

The driver, now wearing a large coat and gloves organised the tickets. Only Two rooms were left un-booked. Albertine decided that it would be best for her to keep close to me, she said it was so I didn't try anything, but I did also have a bomb strapped to my arm, so perhaps she just wanted the chance to talk.

She made me walk up the staircase ahead of her, the stairs creaked and wobbled as we made our way to the top floor, turning left into our room for the night. I sat down on the bed and began to undress folding my clothing as I went. I was unbuckling my belt as Albertine walked in.

"What the fuck are you doing?"

She shut the door, her hands again finding themselves rested on her hips.

"My clothing will look out of place if it's crumpled."

"Who said you were sleeping tonight."

I placed my hands on my hips in imitation.

"Are you propositioning me?"

She didn't blush or smile, just continued to scowl. I felt strangely aroused. At the time I concluded that something was wrong with me, that I could only feel attraction for women who despised me, though as she began to undress, revealing a surprisingly well ordered set of bra and underwear, I realised that I found attractive people attractive.

The gun belt remained in place. I continued to feel at odds with my arousal.

She threw three pillows and a blanket on the floor.

"Get some sleep, wouldn't want your tired skin to give us away."

I weighed up the possibilities, it was unlikely that I could successfully escape, it was also implausible that Albertine would have sex with me. Playing around with various plans for each in my head as I fell asleep.

Waking before dawn, I pulled the blanket off and headed towards the bathroom. Albertine still asleep, held her arm at a right angle, her hand under the pillow, and the corner of the pistol's grip poking out from under the pillow.

The water pressure in the shower was acceptable, I held my head under for a few minutes before I heard the bathroom door open, Albertine stood in the doorway.

"Keeping this open so you don't sneak off."

"You just wanted to see me naked."

"Don't flatter yourself."

She sat down at a table by the bed, looking between me and the sector's streets beginning to animate with life.

I once again dressed myself in front of her, a little self-conscious of what the cool water had done to my manhood.

I joined her at the table, she got up and passed me, entering into the bathroom. Her hands about to grab the doorknob when I interjected.

"Wouldn't want me to sneak off, would you?"

She frowned a little.

"The explosives will take care of you."

"Before I can get help?"

She rolled her eyes and sunk her vision to the floor.

"Sit down, look out the window."

She undressed and proceeded to begin washing herself. The pistol placed on a ledge next to the shower, her left hand hovering motionless above it. I watched her in my periphery. Her abdomen was littered with a few freckles, her skin much lighter than that on her face, the only darker skin was a six inch scar drifting across her abdomen. After a few minutes she returned, we both sat at the table for a few moments, her head was in her arms. Preparing for what was to come.

A half hour later the driver knocked on our door, together we entered the car and drove the half kilometre towards the jail. The driver removed his jacket as he got out, revealing his robotic arm, the black haired Ukrainian then placed a set of handcuffs on his wrists, and together we walked towards the jail. The gates opened and we proceeded. I had entered the building years earlier, procuring the aid of the man whom I named the driver. Only now as I walked through the halls for the second time did I realise that he was a plant. It was always going to be him, one way or another. I had been played. Luckily enough the staff had all changed since my last visit. Only a young twenty something with a few facial scars stood out.

A few guards approached us. The tallest and oldest of the bunch spoke.

"Is he the one?"

The dark haired Ukrainian replied.

"Of course! You see that arm?"

The guard scrunched his nose taking the driver's arm and turned to walk towards the nearest cell block. We all entered. Only five small cells lined the block. It was odd, in my last visit, almost a hundred cells had occupied the other block. Now only six prisoners lay before us. As the lead guard swiped his card Albertine made the move, her silencer already equipped, the first shot went through the leaders temple, the Ukrainian fired twice into the other guards chest, though he managed to recover enough energy to draw his gun, both the Ukrainian and Albertine panicked firing shots into the guards chest. While this was occurring, reacting with the instinct that had served me my whole life, I grabbed at the last man's gun, securing it in a few instances, pointing it flush to the man's skull. Once the commotion was over he stood with hands above his head. I recoiled a little as I watched the bullet tunnel its way through his eyes sockets. Albertine's gun warm in her hand.

The prisoners were unlocked. The driver shrieked at one of them.

"Who the fuck are they, David?"

The man named David, whose face was remarkably familiar spoke both enthusiastic and surprised.

"Friends, people who want to join our cause."

David was the only one of the bunch who still possessed his right arm.

"Have they been re-chipped?"

A pause drifted among the group.

"Yes."

"We only have enough room and anaesthesia for two people! You were meant to be alone!"

A siren began to blur. Of the seven dread filled faces Albertine took the hands of only one, David. Two of the older inmates pushed forward a girl only fourteen years old. I held onto her arm behind my back as I opened the door, firing two shots, incapacitating a guard. Together we formed a triangle around the two civilians working our way to the entrance. All in all sixteen shots were fired, three more guards killed.

In the van the driver revealed himself to be the field surgeon. Albertine drove as fast as she could. The surgeon asked for my assistance, I reluctantly obliged. Holding David and the girl down as they were injected, followed by the dreadful sound of the power saw tunnelling through their flesh and bones. The blood sprayed everywhere, pooling in the corrugated contours and pockets of the van. The surgeon placed a metal disk where their arms had previously been. The disks sealed the wounds, while recirculating and cleaning their blood. I.Vs and blood packs inserted into their shoulders. The remainder of the journey the surgeon held his blood soaked hands over his face, praying for their survival.

The van entered a tunnel in Sector 15, exiting out into Sector 30, entering another tunnel in Sector 33. We arrived in Sector 39 a few hours after lunchtime. I carried the now armless girl to the makeshift hospital, another surgeon and nurse already waiting to complete the operation. The whole incident left me surprisingly hungry.

In the makeshift cafeteria, I asked Duncan when I should expect to have the watch removed, he informed me that it was just a watch, before erupting into a roar of laughter.

Chapter 18

It had been a few weeks since David was rescued. Every evening he, Albertine, Duncan, the typist, would sit down for a meeting in one of the halls of the facility that I now knew to have previously housed a train museum. Occasionally the Ukrainian and I were allowed to sit in on these meetings, plans for the future were discussed at noisome, and David would provide his journalistic secrets, all too often lingering on little titbits that no one else believed to be interesting. The closer he got was pointing out that the name '*Dissented Patriots,*' was not in reference to a Thomas Jefferson quote but actually some self-help writer. No one seemed to care.

On occasions which I was invited to such meetings I would shed whatever insight into the City's operation as I could. It turned out I absorbed a lot of information in the many years of pretending to do things.

By this time I was allowed some degree of freedom. My door no longer locked, I was able to enter the cafeteria and makeshift lounge rooms. On occasion I was permitted to help out in the kitchen. However my leash was only as long as the building. I had begun to miss the unfiltered light.

The young girl turned out to be rather pleasant company. She was rash, moody and sarcastic. Outfitted with two mechanical arms, she would occasionally sneak into my room, to see the 'bad man,' in the following weeks we would often talk. She would steal me novels from the makeshift school that the revolutionaries had set up. The two had become fast friends, sharing a cynical nature and a dark sense of humour.

"How come you get two *roboarms*? David just has the one."

"They're making an example of me. They take me into the Jungle every other day, parade me around, and use me as a recruiting tool."

"How do you like them?"

"My new arms or our great revolutionaries?"

They both smiled.

"Either."

"The arms are interesting, I can do 50 push-ups now, so that's neat. Duncan seems O.K. and what's happening to us is pretty fucked up. So I can kind of forgive them for their…behaviours."

"How's the recruitment drive going?"

"Not too well. Couple of gangs have joined the cause but as you can imagine, they aren't the best or most pleasant allies."

"I think many of our neighbours would say the same thing about myself."

"Maybe you overestimate the savagery of you nature."

"*My-my,* I'm impressed, it seems that school is actually teaching you a thing or two."

"Not really. Just figured, if we're starting some sort of revolution; may as well try to talk proper."

I laughed at the insight of her statement.

"What do you think they'll do with you, once this is all over?"

"I don't think this will ever really be over, but I suppose they'll give me some sort of trial."

"Will they kill you?"

"They won't intend to, at first."

"Then what?"

"I'll force their hand."

"Why would you do that?"

I gave her question the thought it deserved. Since birth, since my first breathe I had been stubborn, whatever I saw of the future, the future would become.

"Because it's in my nature."

The girl whose name was Lucy smiled as she departed. She would join me every evening for a few hours of conversation or silent reading, either way we fuelled each other's stained spirits. This continued for many weeks until one day it was David knocking forcefully on my door

As it turned out David was familiar to me, I was the one responsible for his incarceration. He was the journalist with the dominatrix fetish. David staggered inside, his eyes wide, he was wearing a suit jacket, the right sleeve of which dangled freely. He gestured for me to remain lying on my bed. He pulled up the chair, then proceeded to stare at the ground for a few minutes, the smell of scotch seeped from his pours.

"It was you?"

He slurred out the question, his eyes now glaring lazily at me.

"Yes. Me."

"If it wasn't you it would have been someone else."

It was a statement, though I approached it as a question.

"Probably."

He held out his remaining hand, I took it and we shook left hands. It was strange.

"But, you can't understand what I went through. What you put me through."

The words became louder and more slurred. Before he attempted to punch me in the face, missing by a few inches, losing his balance and collapsing onto the floor.

"Fuck!"

I helped him up. Deciding it was in my best interest to attempt to pry out some information while he was still inebriated.

"David, what aren't they telling me?"

He gave it some thought, staring at the ground again. He seemed as if he was about to say something, but only laughter produced itself from his lips. He took a few moments to get to his feet and exit the room, laughing as he went. I could still hear him from the corridor.

"Hey David, how's the writing going?"

He was almost twelve paces from my door, his reaction took a second but when it came it was easily heard.

"Fucker!"

I closed my door and got beneath the covers, chuckling as I fell to sleep.

When I awoke Albertine was sitting on the chair David had occupied the previous night. She was reading one of a few books stacked on my desk, mostly smuggled from the library.

"Good morning Harry. Ready for another adventure?"

"Well the last one went so great. Why not."

She almost smiled, together we got up and exited the room, and she passed me two bags, the first plastic, too light to hold a uniform. It was a sandwich and a bottle of water. The second bag was filled with the long awaited costume, Albertine let me change in a nearby bathroom. At first glance I thought perhaps the suit was a sick joke, it reminded me of what was once called a gimp costume. It looked like a wet suit with a few pieces of tech attached to the chest and neck. A note at the bottom of the bag read 'Thermo signature dampener.' It took a few minutes to get on, made from a strange, harsh rubber. I half expected a crowd to be gathered ready to laugh at my stupidity once I exited the room. Though I only found Albertine already in her garb, looking significantly nicer than myself.

Arriving at the Garage area, a black car covered in what seemed to be the material as our suits, waited for us. Albertine entered the driver's seat, I, the front passenger. Entering the tunnel system once again, the drive took a little over an hour. On occasion we would be forced to wait in the tunnels due to drone presences in the area. Throughout the trip, Albertine drove in silence, I attempted conversation, only to be denied by her lack of interest.

"What's the outside world like?"

"It's fine."

"Where were you born?"

"France."

"Specifically?"

"Does it matter?"

I gave up. Forcing myself to be contented with silence.

We arrived at a small bunker made from non-printed bricks. Weeds and shrubbery clung to the walls. Albertine grabbed a bag from the boot, reaching inside she handed me my old 9mm. It was a happy yet puzzling reunion. I starred at the grip as I took my possession back.

"Am I trustworthy now?"

"Duncan thinks so, but right now I need you armed."

She used an access code to open the lock on the door, the lock much more current than the building itself. The inside filled with a serious of computers of various makes and ages. Dust and mould littered almost every inch of the room. Albertine placed a device on the newest of the computers, then handed me a circular object, asking me to leave the room and watch for drones on what was apparently a radar. It would take thirty minutes for her to complete her operation. Once she did we drove halfway back to the base. I didn't even try to speak in the car. Arriving at the entrance to the last tunnel, we exited and climbed up a nearby hill. The journey took twenty minutes, though the climb was steep and I had no awareness of where we were going. Eventually, we arrived close to the apex of the summit, from this height the outer wall of the city was visible in the distance. We ate our lunch and drank water as we waited. The boredom ate me up inside, I longed for her to start screaming at me, just to bring some energy and vigour back into life.

"Why did you even come to The Kingdoms?"

"People needed help. I thought I could help."

The words drifted off into the afternoon sky before erupting kilometres away in the background. Hundreds of tiny explosions, occurring all throughout the Jungle.

At this site Albertine got back on her feet, returning to the car. The engine already running by the time I got in my seat. The rain began plummeting, thunder blending into the sound of distant explosions. As we drove Albertine was once again silent.

"What the fuck just happened?"

Silence.

"What was that?"

Silence.

I grabbed at the steering wheel Albertine smacked my hand away, pulling her gun on me as she began to slow down, I knocked it from her hands in a swift slapping motion, the gun now in my hands pointed at her temple. I let it linger for a few seconds, producing no discernable fear in the young woman. In futility I threw the gun into the back seat.

"Just drive."

The quiet was all the more infuriating this time though I stomached it, clenching my jaw and trying to keep the questions out of my mind for a few minutes. Occasionally I would glance back towards her. Steel faced and determined. For the first time since we had met, I began to fear her.

Things escalated substantially once we arrived back at the base, Duncan was waiting outside in the rain, assault rifle in hand, David a few feet behind looking distraught. Albertine stopped a metre in front of the two. Exiting the car unarmed she walked towards them. Now much closer Duncan's rage was evident. I exited the car a few seconds later.

"What the fuck was that?"

Duncan roared.

Albertine continued to stride towards the building. Duncan pulling forcefully on her wrist as she attempted to pass by. He repeated the question.

"What, the fuck, was that?"

She remained silent. David then began yelling.

"We said no! We agreed Al! Do you understand what you've done?"

Finally she turned towards him.

"Sacrifices need to be made. They won't be able to ignore us now!"

"'Us?'"

"Fuck off, David!"

This time they allowed her to move back into the building. David and Duncan following after a few seconds, inside I was eager to get changed out of the wet rubbery costume, though David pulled me aside grasping at my neck with his only hand.

"Do you know what you just did?"

I grasped at his elbow, applying pressure, taking advantage of having two hands.

"No actually, mind explaining?"

I tossed him towards the wall. Duncan observed us from a few meters away. His voice cracked as he addressed me, attempting to supress the anger.

"Get changed, you'll be briefed in ten."

I returned to my room, still completely boggled as to what was going on. As expected the rubber suit took even more effort to remove especially now that it was saturated. I returned to my simple shirt and pants. Moving back towards the meeting room. David, Duncan and Albertine already screaming at one another, the typist nowhere to be seen. I took a seat and waited for their words to return to coherency. It took much longer than I expected. Duncan started us off.

"Harry, you deserve to know what occurred today. The facility which you arrived at was once the emergency broadcast channel for the wider London area. It is now one of a few media channels and one of the only areas in the country with unrestricted internet access. Months ago we learnt that this facility was set for destruction. Once the attacks began this order was put off while your people scrambled to save themselves. After weeks of deliberation. It was decided that we would use this facility to send a manifesto of war crimes to various governments. When you arrived in our laps we learnt of the American, Texan, Chinese and Australian government's support of *The Chairman*. So we added to our manifesto and planned to upload it to the public."

Albertine interjected, throwing her hands in the air in frustration.

"And we did!"

Duncan snapped back at her by continuing his exposition, now faster and louder.

"You escorted Albertine to the facility where she uploaded the documents, however she also uploaded some of the documents and videos to the emergency channel, cutting in to all the screens in the Jungle and the city. Riots ensued. Hundreds of thousands are dead and the number is going up by the minute."

Duncan starred at the ground, Albertine and David both with their faces in their hands.

"So Texas finally seceded?"

David turned red as soon as he processed what I had said, filled with contempt he punched me across the chin, I didn't attempt to avoid it.

"Good jab."

My blood dribbled onto the table.

"So, what now?"

"I don't know."

Duncan admitted, mournfully.

"I do."

We all lifted our heads, surprised by Albertine's statement.

"My people have been preparing. I've made contact, they'll be here tonight."

Duncan let his head drop against the table.

"How?"

"Clearing through the access routes in the channel tunnel. As well as drone support later on."

"How many?"

"Four hundred. Armed and ready. This is what we wanted!"

"How many will die?"

She paused for a moment.

"As many as it takes."

"Do you have a plan?"

"Yes."

Albertine then spent the next three hours explaining the exact details of her design. Duncan contacted his people all throughout the Jungle, organising lieutenants and squadrons. The strategy was split into three separate objectives. Albertine's people would come in and clear a way into the city. The Ukrainian would take a few soldiers and attempt to disrupt the drone operation centre in Sector 8. Duncan and a large force of *Dissented Patriots* would attempt to take the city, lastly I was left with the responsibility to capture the *Chancellor* of Epsilon. Once all of these objectives were complete, we would all converge on Sector 1, to dispose of *The Chairman*, and most likely the many others who stood in the way.

An armoury of weapons were brought out into the main hall, all able-bodied men were asked to take a weapon. I grabbed some armour, a 10mm pistol, some grenades and explosive charges, figuring whatever else I needed could be scrounged off the freshly dead.

Together Albertine and I drove to one of the nearby tunnels. Two hundred armed soldiers were waiting inside busses and armoured vehicles. The explosions continued in the distance, now louder and more rapid in succession, drone fire drowning out the sound of the thunder. As a unit the convoy sped off towards the city, 50.cal turrets pointed towards the sky. On occasion drones would sweep in and attempt to dispatch vehicles. The resulting fire fights chilled my spine. There was nothing I could do but pray to the god I didn't believe in. Only a few of the attempts were successful. In total 12 military drones were shot down by the time we arrived in Sector 12.

The Outer Wall was already destroyed by the legions of makeshift organic grenades, continually raging into the perimeter. Most of the convoy continued into the Outer City, speeding toward the Inner Wall. The roads were stacked with dead bodies and the ruins of the surrounding buildings. The enemy ground forces were in shambles, stumbling through the streets, our forces mowed many down. The Inner Wall was vastly better protected. Sentry turrets, sniper fire and mortars rained down upon us. The explosions consumed many lives. Cars in front and to my left erupted into balls of fire, the smoke consuming all. I dived out the door, declining a look back to check on Albertine. I managed to avoid the snipers as I raced through the smog towards the wall. Crouching in an alcove, I watched as many men from both sides faded from existence, some erupting into great explosions leaving almost no trace of their existence.

I planted bars of explosives upon a weakened part of the structure. The blast allowed for a space wide enough for me to slip through. The battle raged behind me, the backs of the mortar crews in my sight. I could have fired upon them, perhaps killing a few and disrupting there efficiency, thereby saving the lives of some of Albertine's men. It was also likely that I would miss and be shot down where I stood. So I turned my back on the dying men, skulking through the city streets.

The building was blacked out, the power diverted. I placed a charge on the door. The explosion shattered the reinforced bulletproof glass. I entered the lobby, moving towards the emergency stairwell. A few charred bodies littered the flooring, men and woman none recognisable, lying in grotesque, lifeless, obscurity. The stairwell was much the same, blood and char painting the walls.

Every few floors I would explore the offices and hallways looking for signs of life. As I made my way through the building it was clear that the guards had been pushed to the front lines. Though the power had been cut off, generators would boot up in a matter of minutes, directing power to wherever management was occupying. The generators were on the eighth floor, waiting for them to turn on. After a few moments of waiting they began to hum with life. Power was being directed to two floors, the thirtieth and the forty-second. I placed a charge on the generators before manually rerouting power to the elevators. Pistol in hand I pushed the button for the thirtieth floor. In a matter of seconds I was back in halls that had once been my begrudging bore of an office. No lights were on though as I began to walk around the sounds of nervous breathing permeated from a nearby office, entering I found Monica sitting in the dark of the office, an automatic pistol in her left hand, her right arm severed at the elbow, wrapped in bandages, dripping blood. The computers dull light partially illuminating her pale face. She lowered her gun.

"Did you know?"

Monica starred at me blankly. I repeated the question.

"Did you know it was all a lie?"

She continued to stare vacantly. More droplets of blood fell from her bandage. I pointed my pistol at her forehead.

"Did you know?"

"Just take this and hold me."

She held out her shaking arm, a small driver in hand. I took it from her and placed it within my pocket. By this time she had collapsed onto the floor. I Sat next to her, propping her against the wall, an arm around her shoulders. We didn't speak. I just sat next to her as breathing became increasingly fainter. At the time I considered leaving her, she didn't deserve my absolution, though I found myself immobilised, overcome with some strange need to comfort Monica as she faded from existence. The second I knew she was dead, I exited the room and returned to the elevator. I could have looked back, could have stayed there for some time, holding my hand against her skin as it turned cold, but she was dead and it wouldn't have made any difference.

I entered the elevator, heading to the forty second floor. The only light coming from underneath the reinforced door which lead to the communications room, I detonated the charges in the generator room. The lights went dark. I then placed my last two charges on the door, stepping back a few paces before hitting the detonator, the explosives burned through the doors frame, the door fell forward into the room. The approach was far from subtle but I didn't have many options, I threw two flash bangs in before I entered. The room was 20 meters wide and 30 meters long, computer stations throughout, staggered downward like a theatre.

Three men were guarding the *Chancellor*, a fourth already crushed beneath the door. I fired off six shots, managing to kill two of the others while they were still incapacitated. The last guard took cover in the bottom row of the room, the *Chancellor* a few meters behind. I sat in cover while he fired a clip from his SMG, I picked up his squashed partners gun. Getting out of cover I fired the shots in staggered bursts, all the while negotiating my way down the staircase. The decline took almost a minute until finally there was only one row between us I waited, the guard expected me to pop out of cover for the kill shot though instead a computer out of its place in the desk allowing a small clearing with view of the guard's legs, by the time he had noticed, three bullets had torn through his quadriceps. He went into shock in a second.

The *Chancellor* was visibly shaking, clinging to the floor like a child. I pulled him to his feet before forcing the stock of the gun into gut causing him to topple over back onto the ground.

"I want to know everything."

The *Chancellor* lay there trembling, I expected the man to soil himself though to his credit he remained dry throughout our interaction.

"You wouldn't believe anything that I told you."

The communicator on my belt began to beep. I retrieved it, placing it within my ear, Duncan was on the line.

"Have you retrieved *The Chancellor* yet?"

"Yep."

I closed an eye and aimed at *The Chancellor's* groin, kicking the barrel of my finger toward the ceiling in an imitation of gun fire.

"Is he alive?"

"For now."

"OK. Well, we've almost taken the city. Please ask him kindly, if there is anything we need to know heading into Sector 1? If you're satisfied with his answer, feel free to let him go."

Sector 1 was an oddity in a peculiar world. Very few were ever allowed access to the Sector only occupied by *The Chairman's* residence. The house was a mystery. The walls around the property stood so high that the building was not visible, even from the Epsilon roof or any of the other city buildings.

"My boss, my new boss that is, says that we can let you go if you help us navigate our way through Sector 1."

"How am I meant to help you?"

"Well you've been there before haven't you?"

"Once or twice but, I don't recall all that much."

I knelt down and placed the barrel to his forehead.

"Anything?"

"It's only three stories, the building is Victorian, though the basement has been modified and he would most likely be somewhere on that floor."

He blurted the words out, barely coherent.

"Well I guess that is something."

I relayed the message to Duncan, the sound of cannon fire audible in both the communicator and my ears. He then told me a car would be waiting.

"You'll let me go then?"

"Yes but there's no way you'll survive. We've taken the city, and everyone knows your face."

I picked up the guards sidearm exiting the clip.

"One in the chamber."

I trained my gun on him as I walked sideways up the staircase. I was already in the fire escape by the time the shot rang out.

The stairs took a near eternity. The grey concrete monotony drove me close to insanity. Eventually I arrived at the street, entering the military vehicle, I was driven to Sector 1. The streets were cracked, craters everywhere, the buildings stood lopsided, crumbling. The wall to Sector 1 had already broke down before I arrived, large segments of concrete and steel lay in great piles upon the ground. Duncan and Albertine stood meters behind a great blockade of soldiers and military vehicles trained on the *Chairman's* house.

I exited and walked towards them.

"Anyone come out?"

Duncan answered my query.

"No one, the staff must have fled. There could be guards still inside."

"Why haven't you stormed the place yet?"

"We're hoping he'll give himself up."

"Or maybe he's dealt with himself already."

"Maybe."

"I suppose that wouldn't hurt the cause."

"I suppose it wouldn't."

I looked around, the rain had stopped though the streets were still damp with the blood of both sides. Concrete dust drifted through the slight breeze, drifting into the lungs of the soldiers, sweat dribbled down their solemn faces, standing silent in small crowds. The quiet after the storm lasted only a few moments longer. The sound of static drifted from unseen speakers. Slowly the crackle turned to voice. *The Chairman* began to address the crowd.

"It appears I have been bested. Though not just yet."

The sound was similar to the swarming of bees, eight small machine gun equipped drones circled around the crowd of soldiers, and the soldier's intern drew their weapons, pointing toward the sky. The drones could be shot down, though in the fire fight most would lose their lives. After the dramatic tension had reached its crescendo, the audio continued.

"I would formally like to invite the leaders of your terrorist cell in for a little chat. You may bring your weapons on the condition that you bring Mr Neals. You have two minutes."

Duncan looked both confused and alarmed. He pressed a button on his communicator and a moment later Albertine appeared.

"Where is Daniel?"

"His communicator is offline, I think he's dead."

They both hug their heads in a solemn solute. Both were displeased by my interjection.

"Who the fuck is Daniel?"

They both starred at me, Albertine infuriated, her face scrunched up in a frenzy, Duncan just looked like a father who just realised his son was a monster.

"The Ukrainian, Harry. His name was Daniel."

"The Ukrainian is dead?"

"Yeah, Harry, He's probably dead."

Albertine, decided to give her two cents.

"Do we really have to bring Harry?"

"I suppose so."

Walking towards the housing I realised that I had no grasp of what was occurring, a feeling which I should have become accustomed to by now. Duncan held a powerful revolver in his hand, Albertine was grasping an S.M.G. The light of the enflamed city began to fade as we moved closer. Soon we reached the darkness of the entryway. We stood in front of two twin great oak doors.

"There's no doorbell."

"Shut the fuck up, Harry."

"What's up her butt? Oh right, mass murder, slavery and stuff."

Duncan agreed with Albertine.

"Shut up, Harry."

The doors folded open, revealing an unfurnished ballroom, fifty square metres of polished wood floors, Bach played quietly from beneath the flooring. We followed it, leading to a set of stairs, one by one we descended into the basement

The Chairman, at the head of a large dinner table, a red uncooked slab of bloody meat lay in front of him, an empty bottle of wine next to a half empty glass.

"Sit, please."

I was the first to oblige, sitting directly opposite *The Chairman*, the two others eventually sat on either side of myself. *The Chairman* sighed for a few moments before he spoke. Pointing to each of us as he listed our names.

"Duncan, Ms Albertine and Harry."

An extra layer of emphasis was placed upon my own name, it felt rather uncomfortable.

"What is it you want?"

Duncan asked.

"That's not important right now, first I think we should get better acquainted, and how old are you Mr Neals?"

"Thirty-six, personally I think I look closer to thirty-five."

Albertine jerked uncomfortably in her seat.

"Get to the point, old man."

"Harry why don't you get that driver out of your pocket?"

He pushed a small tablet across the table.

"Don't touch that, Harry!"

Albertine got to her feat. I touched it, then placed the driver inside. The driver held many files, one of which automatically opened. A video of a medical procedure, a skinny, gaunt man lay on a table, void of any hair, I skipped further into the video, scientists in lab coats injected large needles into the man's neck, arms, legs, wrists and back. The man was then left on the table, slowly the man's body began to morph and disfigure itself into a more muscular, younger body, and hair growing out of the man's newly rejuvenated skin. The man looked astonishingly similar to myself. I opened the second document.

"You should read this first."

The document was infuriatingly short. Though it shed the insight I never knew I was looking for.

'Test Subject Name: Charles Ryan

Born: 2044

Physical Condition: Below Average

Eye colour: Green

Previous studies conducted in this field have proven successful (Jones & Ames, 2056), those studied showed that some alteration in identity and personal history is possible, however never to the extent that we are planning to perform.

This procedure will investigate whether a total wipe of personality is possible as well as whether a new personality can be programmed into the wiped human brain. False memories, body reconstruction and enhancements, made possible through stem cells will change Charles, a weak feeble medical professional into a hardened and brutish killer.

If the experiment is successful, these procedures will continue, applied within private military.'

"What does is say Harry?"

Duncan's tone was filled with guilt. *The Chairman* answered the question for me.

"It says that Harry, really isn't himself."

I didn't understand, I couldn't of. I opened the next document, it was an image of a single woman, in a beautiful wedding dress and fine jewellery, hanging from a street pole outside the Sector 12 Hotel, strands of her auburn hair drifted in the apparent wind; it was the most beautiful and haunting image I had ever seen. I wish I could say I recognised the woman, though I found any memory of her to be absent.

"Did I kill her?"

"In a way, there were others more involved than yourself."

"Who was she?"

"She was once very dear to you."

Duncan looked nauseas.

"They, used you Harry. They fucked with your head, made you evil and cold, just like them."

"And you both knew, this whole time. You used me!"

Albertine slammed a heavy fist against the table.

"We never owed you anything, you killed our people, good people. You destroyed our plans. So yes, we used you, but 'you,' wouldn't exist without these people. Your body would be inhabited by a man named Charles, a good, boring doctor."

The Chairman, looked pleased at the chaos he had created. It made me uncomfortable, I tried to sheathe these feelings, only to realise my response was the direct result of the programming. For the first time in Harry Neals's life, I began to cry. Duncan looked guilty, Albertine stayed stone faced. *The Chairman,* continued speaking.

"I do realise my own destiny, I know I won't be leaving this room, which is my fate. However, your fates are still on the table."

"You seem contented for a man who is about to die."

"It's my place to die. Are any of you familiar with Phillip the Second, or Pippin the Younger?"

"This isn't a lecture. Get to the point."

Albertine slammed the butt of her gun on the table. *The Chairman* continued unimpeded.

"Philip the Second, grew up as a prisoner of Thebes, he was educated and grew up there. Once he returned to his home of Macedon he was made king, after his brothers had died. Throughout his reign he grew and defended his kingdom. In 336 BC, he was assassinated. His son would ascend to the throne, his name was Alexander the Great. Pippin the younger united the Frankish tribes, his son would be known to most of the world as Charlemagne. Are you seeing my point yet? History will not remember me."

I bit.

"You have a son?"

Part III:

The Moth

Part III:

The Moth

He began to scream, the memories burnt through his consciousness at an impossible speed. He held his hands over his face as the tears began to flood. The grief poured out of him, striking his fist against the cold concrete floor. He busted his knuckles, a small droplet of blood and skin lay solitary on the floor, a small knuckle hair lingering within the blood. A sight which brought a slight reprieve to his frenzy. Slowly and cautiously he rubbed his right hand over his left forearm, feeling the individual bristles. The shock was near consuming. He smiled a little, an involuntary smile, then slowly, again with both hands raised towards his head, first confirming his eyebrows, then grasping at the thick hair on top his head. He continued to smile, though still crying, still grieving. He hoped that it was all a dream, all of it, his entire debt life. The memories were far too real.

He was too consumed by the confusion of his situation to notice his surroundings. The room was dark and cold, Charles couldn't shake the feeling of being in a cave, though it appeared to be the ground level of the dilapidated building. The choked rays of light drifted in from a sizable hole in the wall in front of him. A figure stepped out from the darkness, only visible as a silhouette. The figure continued its approach. The sound of his shoes colliding with the pavement began to grow louder and louder as it made its approach. The powerful thuds echoed as the figure produced itself from the darkness. He wore a dark suit with a torn sleeve, black leather gloves gripping a handgun. He was many years older, but Charles recognised him, *The Charming Man*. His face was torn by wide wrinkles scarring his forehead. *The Charming Man*, sat on a block of rubble a few meters from where he lay. Charles hung his head as he confirmed his memories. 'Was watching me die not enough? Does he really have to do it himself?' The impossible questions raged through him, incapable of making sense of the situation he continued in his despair.

"Charles, do you know who I am?"

"Yes."

"Do you know my name?"

Charles felt toyed with, yet his hopelessness forced him into honesty.

"No."

"Good. I'm sorry to have to tell you this, but, Jane is dead. I killed her. I'm sorry. I know that probably doesn't mean much. Her ashes were scattered by the lighthouse in Trinity Buoy Wharf."

The words seemed rehearsed, yet Charles couldn't shake the impression of sincerity. *The Charming Man*, produced a large black luggage bag from behind the rubble, tossing it towards Charles. Charles began to hyperventilate, the shock of the situation still pulsing through him.

"Everything you need is in that bag."

He paused for a moment.

"You know I practiced this in my head a couple of times."

He let out a dry laugh before he placed the gun inside his own mouth.

"Three. Two. On-."

The shot echoed through the room. The bullet tunnelling through his skull, leaving a wide, gaping exit wound. His body collapsed onto the dirty flooring. The red poured out his mouth in a bloody tidal wave, his eyes remained awake for a few more moments until his light faded from existence. His dead eyes left starring into those of Charles. For a few minutes longer Charles sat gazing at the empty shell before him. Even with the excruciating visual of the man's head erupting, Charles felt that he could not be sure of what he had seen. He could not be sure that Jane was dead, though something in him believed *The Charming Man,* this time.

Brushing his legs off, Charles got to his feet, far more stable than he had felt in many years, his gaze lingered on the black bag. He picked it up, walking out into the open air. He immediately knew he was in The Desert. Open fields, leading to dense forests, sprawled out before his eyes. An empty, unlocked car parked in front of him. The exterior of the car was cracked and worn, with small vines weaving across the contours of the vehicle. Charles found a small blue and black butterfly on the back seat, driver's side handle. Making sure not to disturb the creature, he opened the door, throwing the surprisingly light bag into the back seat. He sat on the car's hood for a few moments, trying to calm himself. It came up in a great wave, all of his unease expressed in spew. When he was sure that there was no more, he entered the vehicle and drove off into the distance.

"Do you believe in God, M-"

He was midsentence when the explosion went off, the flash consumed the room. Albertine, Duncan and Harry were thrown from their seats. Harry's ears were ringing, his eyes burning. He lay on the ground in blind agony for some time. Harry was the first to his feet, he placed a hand on the table to stabilise himself, blood slid down his fingers, pooling on the table in front of him, his vision began to blur, barely able to make out the shape of his own fingers. The hearing came back a minute before his vision. He fumbled around trying to find his seat, pulling himself up, he began to hear his own distorted voice shouting their names.

"Albertine! Duncan!"

There was no response. He lay his head against the table, splinters of pain rippled through his brain. He was almost passed out before his vision returned. *The Chairman's* body lay burned and unrecognisable against the far wall, missing both his arms. The room soon filled with smoke. The tablet lay broken on the table, Harry ripped the driver out placing it in his pocket. Albertine and Duncan lay unconscious on the floor, Duncan's good shoulder was badly burnt and bleeding profusely; in a matter of minutes they would die of smoke inhalation. Harry stepped over their bodies as he stumbled towards the staircase. As soon as he began his ascension, the thought struck him, he was programmed to leave them, that's what they wanted. He walked back down to the basement, lifting Albertine over his shoulder, while dragging Duncan by the wrist. She was light, but he was heavy, the process took the better part of ten minutes, he screamed and cursed his way back into the ballroom before dropping them both onto the hardwood flooring. Light headed, he stepped out into the darkness, the buzzing of the drones ran in tandem with the stinging of his ears, they swarmed and circled like angry bees. The soldiers had their guns trained. For a few moments they circled around, Harry could only imagine the tension in the soldier's arms, as each of them prepared to open fire. The stalemate lasted for a few minutes longer, the drones continued to circle, until suddenly they came stiff, floating in the air, the soldiers dropped into firing stances. Hearts beating faster, sweat dripping down their bodies. The drones buzzed before forming a straight line, floating for a moment before speeding off down the street. A lone figure stood a few hundred meters down the road. Harry attempted to make out the figure's details, though the man was a blur, and soon everything else was as well. Harry collapsed, falling backwards back into the ballroom. The three of them lay there, broken, bleeding.

The night raged on for a few hours longer. *The Chairman's* men retreated into the Outer-City, laying low biding their time.

Harry would awake from a coma a week later in the Sector 3 hospital. The hospital itself had received significant collateral damage. Entire wings of the facility had been brought down by mortar fire. The damage in Harry's room was minimal, though, the lighting in his ward was dimmed to a painful yellow glow. A man with a shotgun stood positioned next to him. Lucy sat at the foot of the bed reading. He noticed that her breasts had grown, he scolded himself over the absence of guilt.

"What have you got there?"

"Green Eggs and Ham."

"Aren't you a bit old?"

"I kind of missed out on the whole childhood thing, because you know, crazy dictatorship lies."

"Right. It's nice to see you."

"You too."

She moved up the bed and hugged him, he attempted to hug back but found himself barely able to move.

"A few of your ribs are broken, they also found a piece of the table stuck in your chest, and you lost a lot of blood."

"Your eardrums took some damage as well, though with some help we managed to repair your implants."

Said a doctor in a lab coat that did not quite fit his size. He had just entered the room holding a tablet. He checked on two other patients before coming to Harry's side.

"Implants?"

"Perhaps the child should leave before we have this discussion."

Lucy got to her feet, Harry attempted to grasp at her, groaning as the pain of movement set in.

"Stay."

"Are you sure?"

"No, that's why I think you should stay."

Harry nodded at the doctor, the doctor then placed the tablet in Lucy's hands, she held it so that Harry could see. The display showed a diagram indicating all of the implants and augmentations active within his body. The doctor pointed towards each.

"This one limits lactic acid build up in your muscles, these strengthen your joints and limit strain."

The doctor swiped at the display revealing another diagram showing Harry's brain.

"This regulates your dopamine levels, this one interestingly enough, in your motor cortex regulates your mirror neurons. It appears that without hormone implants you may revert to a state of depression, the mirror neuron changes seem to allow you greater ability to imitate others."

"How did these things get inside me?"

"It would appear that these augmentations were installed several years ago, during the process of your creation."

"His creation?"

Lucy interrupted, looking both confused and angered.

"From the information in our possession, we know a man named Charles Ryan's physical makeup and brain structure were completely altered. The process was achieved through the use of stem cells utilised by a singular piece of highly advanced machinery. We know little of the machine other than the core concepts, the machine was designed to code and shape DNA. We know this machine was commissioned by an individual known only as M. We have some preliminary designs but that's it"

"Monica?"

"I'm not familiar."

"She was my handler."

"Well I suppose she may be responsible, it would appear that you have quite a few enemies."

Harry closed his eyes for a brief moment, his thoughts lost in the memories of Monica, the moments of silence, lust, hatred and malice.

"Is there anything else doctor?"

"My colleagues believe that it would be best to give you information bit by bit, wouldn't want to overload you. One thing I can tell you is that you are actually four years older than you believed. You turned forty yesterday."

The doctor got up and exited the room.

Harry and Lucy were silent for some time, each attempting to process the information, until Lucy broke the silence.

"Happy Birthday!"

Harry smiled, the entirety of his existence was beginning to crumble before him. He wanted to scream, to be violent. Destroy the world and make it as scarred and wrong as he felt. He decided to laugh instead. Lucy laughed as well, only not quite so loud.

"What happened to the others?"

"Who?"

"Albertine and Duncan. Where are they?"

Lucy's face went pale.

"Duncan is in intensive care. They've been working on him this whole time, don't think he'll make it. Albertine, well she's running the show now. Her and her people."

"Her people?"

"Yeah those European guys with the guns, almost half of them survived, they're the ones running this city."

"Who are they?"

"Political activists, people who wanted to leave their old lives behind, for whatever reason."

"And what do our saviours stand for?"

"Well we're communist now, so that's interesting. *The Chairman's* people are still trying to kill us though. "

"*The Chairman* is dead. Who is their leader?"

"*The Chairman* is their leader, well at least the new *Chairman.* "

"I guess that shouldn't be surprising. We're communists?"

"Socialists seems more accurate, it's hard to tell seeing as we're still in this civil war."

"Where do we control?"

"London, the City and the Jungle. *The Chairman's* people have retreated to Liverpool, which apparently still exists."

"Have we received any contact?"

"How would I know? They don't really trust the teen with too much. "

"Does Albertine know I'm conscious?"

"Not yet, it can only be a matter of time."

Harry lifted the sheet from over him, his chest was covered by pressure bandages, and he noticed that he had lost a considerable amount of weight.

"What happened to Daniel?"

"He was killed trying to destroy the drone facility, they recovered his body days ago, before they levelled the building."

Harry felt no sadness to hear of the Ukrainian's death.

"The poor kid."

Heads I win, tails you lose. He had never realised it, but these were the odds running against him his entire life. As a result, these were the odds he gave every government figure that he got his metallic fingers on.

In the February of 2084, Ray had tracked down a jail guard that he had the pleasure of running into in a past life. Bloody scalpel in hand, cutting through the eyelids of the gent, he made the realisation. In truth, Ray had only a hazy memory of the man's impasses against him, though, he knew of their occurrence. He had to be punished. The tissue was far thicker than he had expected. The blood flooded down his face, he screamed, a loud annoying scream, which soon turned to an empty groan, as the shock set in. He watched the man for a few minutes, twitching and drooling the last of his life away. After he was satisfied an assistant handed him the shotgun. Two shots rang out. The man's intestines ripped apart by the shards of metal. He left him there to rot, capturing some level of poetry that Ray didn't quite understand.

He opened a door and walked out into the scorched earth. A city stood crumbling before him, tents and shelters littering the horizon. Somewhere a man was standing over his brother's fresh corpse, somewhere else a baby was screaming, and would never stop. Ray thrived among it all. By this time there was only few of the original *Patriots* left among the fold, looking sad and solemn with their primitive robotic arms. The revolutionaries begun calling themselves *The New Sons and Daughters of the Revolution.* The previous day they had changed it from *The Young Sons of Liberty,* the older and more female of the revolutionaries had a problem with the name, as did those with no grasp of political philosophy. Ray didn't really care what they were called, all he cared about was that they continued the hunt. Ray spent most of his time in the field, though on this cold February morning, other plans took `priory. The U.N. had sent a representative, her name was Sarah Marsh, a short Canadian woman, her hair was shaven into a short Mohawk and her eyes an intimidating bright yellow. Texas sent their own representative, a greying old man who took far too long to finish his sentences. Lastly the C.E.O of an Indian multinational corporation, her right arm substituted by a smooth metal alloy replacement, every few minutes she would check a screen planted in her wrist displaying stock information. The meeting took place in what Ray called the boardroom, but was in fact just a broken industrial sized freezer with a large table inside, Ray enjoyed the silence of the representatives squabbling, a roll of the eyes, an avid stare, and the occasional sigh. After several minutes of the beautiful silence, the U.N woman Sarah Marsh began to address Ray.

"Mr Neals, what you, and your people have suffered through is horrendous, we wish to help make reparations for what was done to your people."

"I am not Mr Neals."

"But Mr Neals is the leader of your... government, isn't he?"

"Yes."

"And you are the leader?"

"Yes."

"So, you must be Mr Neals?"

"I am Mr Sancher."

"Who is Mr Sancher?"

The U.N woman was clearly worried. She drew a communicator from her pocket, scratching at her screen for a few moments.

"Mr Sancher was, Mr Neals."

"So, you are Mr Neals?"

"No I am Mr Sancher, Mr Sancher was Mr Neals."

"And Mr Neals is Mr Sancher?"

"No. Mr Neals was Mr Ryan."

"Right."

She starred at the floor, filled with frustration and tremendous sense of alarm.

"We want to help you and your people thrive."

The CEO then interrupted.

"As are we. We're willing to offer any basic limb augmentation to each of your people."

Her eyes lingered on Ray's augmentations. Her mouth curled into an expression of severe discomfort.

"From what we can tell, your enemy has been utilising some of the most advanced augmentation technologies in the world. It's time to get even."

"Has 'He' been augmenting himself?"

The excitement was clear in Ray's voice, he made no attempt to quell the glee bubbling beneath the surface.

"As far as we know, yes."

"How can you not be certain, you are the only company that makes sophisticated augmentations?"

"Yes."

"So, shouldn't you be able to know whether 'He' is using augmentations?"

"Yes."

"And, is 'He?'"

"We are not at liberty to comment on that, at this time."

"What about you, Mr Texas?"

"I'm here to persuade you not to forfeit the soles of your people. These extended lives are not natural!"

The old man's eyes drifted on the C.E.O's arm

"And, we are all going to hell if we choose the fancy robot arms and organs?"

"Yes, sir."

"How about the horrific bloody uprising?"

"God gives forgiveness to those who ask."

"What if those who ask have augmentations?"

"Augmentations defy what god has planned, it's unnatural."

"What do you give us if we remained…unarmed?"

"Well, nothing. We are not responsible for your misfortunes, it's up to you to save your people's soles."

Ray sighed, burying his face into his hands.

"How many more of these do I have today?"

Ray's assistant rushed to his side and held out a tablet with nearly 100 names, mercenaries, journalists, drone manufacturers, suppliers, buyers, dealers, pacifists, communists, capitalists, evangelicals and atheists. All offering their unconditional support, 'on one condition.' One by one, they flooded into the freezer, screaming at the top of their lungs, shoving screens in the faces of any of the *The New Sons and Daughters of the Revolution,* each of them asking,

"Are you Mr Neals?"

Charles had been lost for some time, if not for the conventional, dull grey sky, Charles wouldn't have believed himself to be in England. The great, stretching fields were ruptured by hundreds of tall concrete towers with vast blocks of solar panels, all facing the hidden sun. Charles drove close to one of the towers, a sign read 'Amos Farm.' Vertical, indoor farms had been in existence for almost fifty years, though Charles had never seen one in person. He felt surprised that such trivialities could still captivate his attention, even with the ominous presence of the black bag. He didn't really know where he was going, the road only ran in one direction, he wondered where he was or even when he was, all he knew was that he had awoken in a world far distant to that in which he had fallen, the landscape was different to that in which he had grown up in, perhaps even more dissimilar to the society of *The Union*. Driving down the road he found no signs of the country he had once known. The rivers were cleaner, the flats and fields now dark sweeping forests. He continued along the long sweeping road, his eyes lighter than he had expected, the confusion and grief turning into adrenaline. He forced the questions out of his mind, trying to focus on the road before him. The sun would soon be setting, he hoped to find some further signs of life before nightfall.

After another half hour, Charles began to spot lights in the distance, great flickering lights littering the horizon, titanic towers filling the skyline. He had found his way to London. The city was unrecognisable from such a distance, buildings appeared where they had never been, the city walls no longer standing. Charles continued down the road, approaching the first building he came across. He stopped at an ugly block of a building, grey glossy concrete, three stories high, a sign on the side read; 'Exit Motel.'

Charles grabbed the bag from the back of the car, hoping there was something inside that could be traded for a room for the night. He zipped the bag open, revealing large stacks of Euros, hundreds of thousands. He grabbed at a few notes before entering into the lobby. A young man with ambitiously stylish hair was sitting at a desk. Charles almost wept at the sight of the young man. The bubbles in his stomach felt cancerous and painful, he half expected the blood to spill through his skin.

"Can I help you?"

"How much for a room for the night?"

"Fifty Euros for our base rooms."

Charles nodded, still overtly confused. He handed over the money. The boy passed a small card. Charles took it and headed for his room on the second floor. Opening the door to reveal a medium sized room with a small bed and a titanic television. Charles placed the bag onto the bed, he was eager to unpack its contents, though he had one thing which he had to do first. He approached the bathroom with heavy feet, his heart pounding faster and faster as he made his approach. He saw a glimpse of the mirror, reflecting the shower behind. He stopped for a moment, attempting to gather himself, he was still unsure about whether he should have just stayed in the desolation that he awoke, lying next to *The Charming Man,* until he was just as dead. He couldn't shake the feeling that he was still being toyed with. He stepped into the bathroom with his eyes closed, he turned to face the mirror. Slowly, ever so slowly he began to open his eyes. The image didn't register for some time. It was as if he could see himself, yet was unable to comprehend what he was seeing. The last time he had seen his reflection he was 34, yet the weight loss, the poor nutrition and the despair had aged him almost ten years. Now the reflection before him was almost unrecognisable, his bags had subsidised, his forehead smoothed, barely any signs of wrinkles. He looked as if he were closer to 25. He touched the skin on his cheeks and his forehead, the soft texture was almost alarming. He stood starring into his own eyes for a few moments before he began to undress the suit shirt that he had woke up in. Button by button he revealed himself. He was in better shape than he had been for a long time, the scars of his message to Claire were no longer there, he traced over the imagined lines, the memory burning in his head. He undressed himself, throwing his brown pants and leather shoes across the room, before entering the shower, running warm water through his hair. He began to weep uncontrollably for Jane. They had been growing apart for some time, he had always been aware of it, but he had loved her and now she was dead and he was stuck in a wave of confusion. He dried himself, wrapping the towel around his waist before continuing back into the bedroom. He looked at the black bag and its mysterious contents, feeling compelled, Charles spilled the bags contents onto the bed. He noticed the money first, nearly a million euros, then the leather-bound notebook, a silver communicator and finally, a solitary paper letter.

He placed the money back into the bag, moving the letter and book onto the bedside table. He was scared to delve inside, yet perhaps more scared to leave the information unattended. The remote was close to hand, he pressed the button and the screen erupted into a news report on an education bill passing through the senate, a small time stamp in the corner of the screen read; '07/07/90.'

Charles realised he had been asleep for twenty years.

An inch square incision had been made in Duncan's skull, three surgeons were inserting various tiny instruments within. Duncan had reduced into a warped, barely recognisable version of himself. The muscular atlas, the distinguished, hardened commander now condensed to a skeletal shell of a man. Harry knew that he wouldn't survive, he hoped he didn't because he wouldn't entirely survive, he would stay a shell. Though these thoughts came too natural, so Harry told himself that he hoped that Duncan survived, hoped he would be just as he was before.

Harry had only been on his feet for a couple of days, physical therapy consisted of walk until you can't walk, then crawl. Now Harry could walk through most of the day before reverting to crawling. He spent hours watching the surgeons operate. Occasionally Lucy would walk with him. He enjoyed her company and thought nothing of her watching their great leader die, as a result of this he made sure to keep her from watching the operation.

"Why are they still going?"

Harry had no answer for her, he had no idea himself.

"Because he is a good man."

"Do you really think so?"

Harry didn't believe in good men, he supposed they had died out long ago, helpless to their own ignorance.

"Yes."

Lucy took Harry's hand and together they walked through the halls of the hospital, every now and then, there would be a crack in the ceiling or the flooring, the occasional blood splatter. Definite safety hazards. The other wards were far more occupied, hundreds of men woman and children being treated for burns and damn near everything else. Many of the doctors and medics working for *The Chairman* had been captured, Albertine forced them to extract the chips from the arms of the civilians. The success rate was relatively high, 92% or so, however, on the scale of hundreds of thousands, it wasn't too long until there were barely any more surgeons left.

Harry ended up in what was once the specialist's wing, arriving at the office of a Dr Stout, PhD in Cognitive Psychology. Stout was a tall man with a solemn face, unusually thin, the German ancestry very prominent. His office was large with many degrees and accommodations lining the scope of the walls. His windows were cracked, a few bullet holes in the upper corners. What was most prominent of all the room's features was the lack of a desk. Only a chair and two other chairs facing one another, a pile of the doctor's possessions lay between them. His eyes were surrounded by dark circles, at a glance one would assume the doctor was sleep deprived though it seemed to Harry that the circles were in fact bruises, from one assault or the other. Harry sat down a few seconds before Stout, his knees sat disturbing high off the ground. Harry let Lucy depart this time. The doctor picked up a folder from the floor, flipping open the contents and perusing the details. His expression stayed perfectly, impossibly level.

"You are quite the enigma Mr Neals."

Harry stayed quiet.

"The higher ups, have decided that you will be, once again a guinea pig."

He said the words with the enthusiasm and meter of a stone.

"Myself, and a group of specialists will be attempting to restore your personality, back to that of Mr Ryan."

"I still don't know Who Charles Ryan is! Why should I become him… again?"

"Some files on Mr Ryan have been sent to your tablet, and may I propose a question?"

Harry nodded as slightly as he could.

"Do you still want to be Harry Neals?"

Harry didn't really see why not.

"No I don't."

"Then we must begin this process."

"Sure."

The doctor turned around, he began to rifle through an ugly ancient filling cabinet behind him. Throwing containers and papers across the room, tax forms, old love letters, finally his efforts amounted to producing a plastic bottle filled with a number of white pills. He tossed it across the ghost desk, Harry caught them and held them to the light, twenty shiny orbs of poison.

"Take two every day."

Harry was suspicious, so he plunged two down his throat in an instant.

"Now what?"

"Now, you go find the fMRI technicians in the basement."

Harry didn't want to. So, he got up eagerly and exited the room, thanking the doctor who he had grown to hate with fury.

Harry found himself back in the halls, walking through the cracked corridors. The thoughts and questions flooded through his mind, he thought it best to shut it off. Then the thought occurred to him, he was trying to act opposite to his own thoughts, an attitude that was a thought itself, coming from inside his brain. He decided it would be best to do the opposite of the opposite of the thing that came most natural, an attitude Harry believed would eat into his day.

Harry entered the stairwell, jogging down the flights of stairs. He believed that he was recovering well, but he questioned this belief, thinking perhaps he wasn't recovering as he should, then questioning that, he decided he was in fact recovering well.

The basement of the building was dark and unnaturally moist, the ventilation hadn't been installed correctly and as result the room was stuffy and uncomfortable. The technician was waiting by the machine, he was a squat man with a chubby body and the type of unshakable smile that in turn brought conflicted smiles to others. Harry didn't like him, though he questioned that belief, and in turn questioned that belief, arriving back at stark dislike for the small Santa like man.

"Get in my friend and we'll begin the program. The air-conditioning will kick in soon."

The man handed Harry a pair of ear buds, he placed them on. Harry approached the arch of the machine sceptically. Harry had heard that such machines had been downsized significantly, though not this one, the machine took up the better part of the room. Harry lay flat on the bed, it clicked as he was taken in to the cramped alcove of the machine. Harry found himself starring at a small monitor, the man's heavy breathing in his ear; it sounded like cholesterol.

"We're just going to run a few test, the machine should start working in a minute."

The machine began to wheeze as a black and white image of a shirtless man popped up on the display, 'Rate how attractive you find this person from 1-7.'

Harry pressed 6, then 2 then 6 again before pressing enter.

'How likely would you be to talk to this person in a social situation?'

Harry pressed, 3, then 3, then 3 again before hitting enter.

The tests ran one by one for over an hour.

'How upset is this person? How much sympathy do you feel? What level of anger does this image make you feel?'

Harry was let out of the machine, the technician handed him a bottle of water. The man's smile was still present, only much smaller, wavering at the corners.

"I sent the results up to the psychologist. He says to see him immediately."

Harry attempted a smile before beginning to exit the room. The technician smiled back, Harry remembered that he didn't much like the technician, though he made himself like him so that he could choose to not like him again.

Harry again walked past all the cracks and bloodstains on his way back to the psychologist's office. Harry couldn't help but wonder what would be next for him? He felt that he had no control, and never did. The psychologist more or less confirmed this when he arrived back in the office.

"Sit down."

Harry thought it would be best to obey and sit, questioning this, he decided to stand, a few seconds later he was sitting in the chair.

"A colleague of mine will be arriving shortly."

The psychologist was staring intently at a tablet he held awkwardly in his lap.

"You are quite the peculiar man, Mr Neals. May I ask? Why did you change your answers to their opposite, then change them back for each score?"

"Well I don't trust my own thoughts, but that is in itself is my own thought, so I do the opposite of the thought I don't trust."

"Which ends you on the original thought?"

Yes, no, yes.

"Yes."

Harry realised the impossibility of evading his thoughts a few moments before another doctor arrived in the room. He sat down next to Harry, his badge read, 'Jade Cameron-Neurologist.' Cameron held at her hand Harry shook it.

"Hello Mr Neals, I'm going to ask you to do something for me."

Cameron dug into her pockets, producing two oranges and a needle with thread. She handed Harry one with the needle and thread.

"Make yours, like mine."

The doctor turned over the side of her orange to reveal a line of stitching.

"I don't understand."

"Just give it a shot, take your time."

Harry observed the stitching pattern for a few moments before he began an attempt, in a few seconds Harry had produced an identical pattern. Both Stout and Cameron sat a little wide eyed. Harry felt similarly shocked.

"What just happened?"

Cameron answered him first.

"Motor learning, it would appear you have retained some motor behavioural ability from your previous existence as Charles Ryan."

"What does that mean for me?"

The psychologist answered this time.

"It means, that some form of Charles Ryan's memory is still present within your brain."

"Could you get any more memories out?"

"Well, we'll try."

The salespeople didn't leave for a month. Ray had already made over a hundred handshakes and signatures. He promised seventy of his most photogenic limbless orphans to a campaign for the Indian augmentation company. The contents of the private art galleries and museums of the dead aristocrats were sold off to the Louvre in Paris and the Natural History Museum of New York. The whole city was again beginning to take its skeletal shape. The *printers* running overtime to produce a gargantuan slum around the outer walls of the City. Order was starting to be born from the chaos. The murder rate was dropping, the hospitals weren't so full. Credits no longer meant anything, as a result motivating people into working was insidiously difficult. The new nations brief stint as a quasi-communist utopia didn't much work out either. Some of the factories were still running, as were some farms in the surrounding areas. The people were being clothed and fed. Since the incident, Ray had become sufficiently adept at surgery, his augmentations made the job much easier, he spent two days a week in the emergency department of the hospital. Now the civilians were living far longer, the major problem was getting them something to do. Ray took it upon himself to train as many willing civilians to become soldier. Hatred of the new *Chairman* was an incredible motivator or excuse for the blood thirsty.

Each weekend he would take the trainees into Liverpool. The helicopter could carry up to ten. Together they would venture through the streets in an attempt to find *The Chairman*'s men and their dugouts. The city was mostly deserted, every few blocks they would run in to small packs of survivors, all of them exceptionally terrified. Occasionally the frightened people would work up enough hatred that they would take action, sometimes they would throw bottles or produce knives, sometimes the cadets would get spooked and fire upon the civilians, sometimes those cadets would get promoted.

Winter had ended and the vagrants had ascended into the light, and there were more of them than Ray had previously believed. They congregated in the craters and streets of the burnt out city. The helicopter buzzed overhead, scanning the buildings for signs of life.

An hour in to the day's search, the helicopter picked up on something, a group of heat signature in the third floor of what had once been a food market. Something glowing was stored in a case by where the group had been standing.

Ray's soldiers stormed the building, breaking down a door and charging up two staircases. *The Chairman*'s people fired first, killing three of the cadets in an instant. Ray returned fire many seconds before any of his underlings, all of them too busy chocking for air or running for their lives. Ray threw tear gas into the corridors attempting to flush them out. Most of his enemies ran out the windows, in an attempt to land on the ledge of the lower floor, though, one enemy soldier ran straight towards Ray. The man charged with a knife, Ray fired a shot which hit the man in the shoulder and brought him to his knees. As the man began to scream, Ray injected the tranquiliser and got out his scalpel. The incision was smooth and the extraction of the man's tag only took a few seconds. He placed a tourniquet on the man's arm and used a lighter to seal the wound. Throwing the man into the possession of his last two cadets. The crates that had been giving off heat were various armaments, including rockets and sniper rifles. It appeared they were to be used on Ray's patrol. He gestured for a cadet to grab one of the boxes. Outside the helicopter landed, the three and their prisoner boarded as the helicopter took off. Ray aimed one of the rockets at the third story of the market, firing as soon as they were sure not to be affected by debris. The explosion ignited the other leftover rockets, causing the flooring to collapse. The prisoner was kept face down, his arms strapped behind his back. He shouted and screamed in an eastern European accent. Ray pressed his shin uncomfortably against the man's ribcage. He continued to rage and squirm, Ray then slapped him across the back of the head with the barrel of his gun. The man collapsed to unconsciousness.

The journey took less than an hour. It was an incredibly clear day, blue sky with solitary clouds drifting in the distance. Below, the land was cut and torn, the damage of the civil war had disfigured the landscape. Old towns had been overrun by the grasp of nature, old cobbles bursting with great oaks and shrubbery. Nearby fields turned into sprawling forests, landmines littering the undergrowth of these forests. Ray never knew who dropped them, all he knew was people would try to leave the cities; that these people often erupted in the night, into harshly beautiful explosions, lighting up the distance. From the helicopter, Ray spotted the little craters, standing out from the fauna. Trees and people fell, and Ray knew they made a sound.

Back in London, they radioed ahead, landing in the military base that had once been the *Patriots* headquarters. Ray had an office in the city, however he preferred to take any meetings at the base, with all of his dirty secrets within reach. Ray escorted the prisoner to the make shift cell block, which had formerly occupied the civilians. A medic arrived and extracted the bullet from the prisoner. Once the medic left, Ray closed the door, locking them both inside.

The prisoner had been stripped of the dirty combat armour that he had no doubt been wearing for multiple weeks. In some manner these cells were better accommodation than they soldiers had been used to for some time. Though now the prisoner was alone, in the dark, with Ray, a six inch blade in Ray's hand.

The restraint was only a few kilometres down the road, tucked between two colossal farming towers. The establishment was almost completely empty by the time Charles arrived, he was directed towards a table in the corner of the room, the waiter retrieving the unused cutlery which sat opposite where Charles was seated. The waiter left a small tablet displaying the menu before returning to the kitchen. Charles thanked the waiter as he walked away. Charles didn't much care what he ordered, he knew anything would taste exceptional after all that he had been through. He ordered a '300 Gram L.G Rib Eye. Medium Rare,' and a scotch. He had no idea what the 'L.G,' stood for but he was ravenous none the less. He withdrew the letter and notebook from his pocket, the excitement shrank away. He had not yet explored its contents, too scared of what he might find. He opened the letter revealing an A4 page, handwritten, a small paper square drifted out of the bottom, tumbling to the floor. Charles retrieved it, turning it around to reveal a small picture of Jane. She was wearing a red dress with matching red lip stick, standing on the balcony of a building in the City. She was more beautiful and happy than he had ever seen her before. A tear glided down the side if his face in response. He gathered himself before beginning to read.

'I'm sorry, Charles. You did not deserve the life that was inflicted upon you. You deserved the life that you will now live. I know things will never be the same, but you can have a future now, you can make the world better place. The notebook's pages will outline your new life. All of the details, accounts and information. You will have many questions, I cannot answer them all, for your sake, mostly.

I am now departed from this world, your revenge stripped from you. I am not trying to make excuses, but I think you should know, this was always going to happen, I was sick. I was born with a sickness beyond my control. I apologies for all the lives I ruined.

I wish you the best of luck with the rest of your existence.

With regards, and deep admiration;

M.'

Charles finished the letter as the waiter arrived with the plate of food. Charles was a little startled by the speed that the food had arrived. A concern that soon passed when he registered the incredibly enticing smell of the meal. He again thanked the waiter as he departed the table. The steak was accompanied by potatoes, steamed vegetables, and a peppercorn sauce. The waiter returned once more with Charles's scotch, placing it on the table, the waiter then placed a small white pill next to the glass. Charles starred at it puzzled. The waiter again began to exit. Charles called after him.

"Excuse me, sir. What is this?"

Charles held the pill between his fingers, the waiter stood starring, with his eyes wide.

"It's a vitamin and nutrients booster. We have to give them out with every meal. I'm sorry, I thought you were from around here?"

"I am, I've been away for a while."

The waiter laughed.

"Probably for the best."

Sensing that Charles was still tense, the waiter retrieved another tablet from a dispenser on his belt, placing it in his mouth.

"Just don't have more than ten a day and they'll keep you well nourished."

Charles swallowed the tablet, washing it down with a sip of scotch.

"Anything else that I can help you with?"

Charles blushed, a little embarrassed. He supposed that he better get used to the confusion.

"What does 'L.G,' stand for?"

"Lab grown, that beef steak was never inside a cow."

The waiter left Charles to eat his meal. He was suspicious at first, though after a moment he realised that it would be the greatest meal of his life so far. As he ate, he flipped through the pages of the notebook, an apartment had been purchased in his name in London's West End. He wondered whether it was a trap. Perhaps he would arrive their only to once more fall into the grasp of *The Charming Man.* He tried to force the thoughts from his mind until he had finished his meal.

After a few minutes he was finished and the check arrived, he handed over the money.

The waiter smiled.

"Have a good night."

"You too."

Charles drove back to the motel. He took a shower. He sat under the water, stupefied, tracing the skin on his arm where his tag had once been.

Eventually he snapped out of it, dragging himself into bed. He waited for sleep to consume him, the clock displayed on the TV monitor taunting him with every passing hour. It was 3am before Charles gave up. Gathering his things he left the room, placing the key card at the reception desk. Exiting the building, walking out into the illumination of the stars. He threw the bag into the back seat. Turning on the communicator he placed the address of the Trinity Buoy Wharf. The roads were far more intricate than they had ever been in Charles's life, though after a few minutes of studying the map he took off, his headlights ignited the road leading to the mysterious metamorphosis of the city that he had always lived in.

Harry had been receiving treatment for two months. Building on his muscle memory, beginning to preform basic surgeries. Once he observed a procedure he would be able to emulate it near instantly, during these procedures Harry was unable to explain his actions. Many of the hospitals staff objected to Harry working there, though there were far too few able bodies for the management to turn down a spare pair of hands. During the evening, Harry would answer a series of questions as Charles Ryan, yet he found that he was no closer to becoming him. In actuality, he didn't much like Charles, he seemed a fool. Someone too small and weak, a man who allowed himself to be eaten and digested by the world, then spat out as a shade. Not much was known about the man, only pieces of information gathered from former associates or colleagues, the man didn't really have any friends. He was a surgeon, completing his degree through an accelerated program, he worked as a surgeon for a number of years, once *The Union* 'took over,' he chose to live in poverty. Chose to be poor and meek and insignificant. He allowed himself to be crushed.

Harry's only real hope of changing was to find M, find whatever machines they used to create him. The war continued to rage onward and no information had come up. Harry and Albertine were still yet to cross paths, though he would see her on television from time to time, the unquestionable leader of London, making deals, shaking hands. A few thousand more Europeans had made their way to London, socialists, communists, liberals, those fleeing their existences, all hoping to get in on the ground floor of a nation. Finally after weeks of being the leader of this flock, she had made contact with him. Through Lucy, he was informed of a lunch meeting to be held in the Sector 1 house.

By this time Harry had been out of the hospital for weeks. He was back living in his old apartment, the real apartment. Twelve others were living in the fake apartment next door. He could hear them when he got close to the fireplace, hear those slurring drunken, melancholy half sentences or the sound of them eating like animals, or fucking like the human animals that they were. They didn't know he was there listening and living alongside them, he would come and go through the emergency exit. Only Lucy knew, she would sleep on the couch most nights, they would eat together and watch the movies that Harry had stored on his entertainment system. They had spent the previous evening watching *2001 A Space Odyssey*.

"The C.G.I. in this is terrible!"

Lucy exclaimed, chunks of pie mince tumbling out of her mouth.

"This was made before C.G. It's all practical effects."

"Holy shit!"

More mince sprayed onto the carpet.

"How did they do that?"

"I have no idea."

"What is this movie even meant to mean?"

"I have no idea."

"Kind of predicted the future wrong."

"I think almost everyone does. Optimists see rainbows, pessimists see dust. Absurdists see whatever they want."

"What are absurdists?"

"People who do not believe in purpose."

He stopped the movie, sensing the discussion was likely to press on for some time.

"So, nothing is absolute?"

"Too them, yes."

"Then what about the principle itself."

Harry regretted the theatrics of his earlier statement, the conversation was becoming frustrating but he didn't know why.

"What principle?"

"That nothing is absolute."

He didn't really care.

"I suppose so."

"Why did you even mention absurdists?"

"Just something I've been thinking about."

"Why?"

"I honestly have no idea."

That's when she told him that Albertine wanted to meet. He considered that she was too young to be so central to the uprising, he was no longer sure what to do with this thought and all the others he had. They would spend the rest of the evening watching films and eating too much food.

Harry dressed himself in a suit and hopped on a makeshift bus headed towards Sector 1, the bus was small and cramped, thirty sweaty bodies, all standing up, bumping against one another in the unventilated steel. An old man with a dirty beard shuffled towards him, his hand outstretched.

"Have a spare food coupon."

Now that communism had swept the nation the only way to acquire food was through government coupons. A system that only worked for a few days before it was corrupted, those responsible for handing out the coupons only did so if there was something in it for them, and fake coupons were being forged by the second.

As the old man approached, Harry felt a slight tickle by his trousers pocket, he reached into his jacket, quickly withdrawing his pistol, in one motion he slapped the old man with the barrel of the gun, then quickly turning his body around to strike a young man behind. The young man fell to the floor, Harry's wallet in hand. Kneeling down and retrieving it, Harry got off the bus at the next stop, then walked three blocks, arriving at Sector 1. The building had been repaired and repainted after the explosion, a flag pole sat in the courtyard, a black rectangle with three solitary triangles of gold staggered across.

A military policeman stood outside the door, the same strange flag embodied on the chest of his uniform.

"We were told that you would be armed, please relinquish any firearms and prepare for a pat down."

Harry winced when the man referred to himself as 'we.'

"You can pat me down, but you're not taking my gun."

The guard grasped at a small communicator on his chest calling for backup. Five other guards materialised behind him. All of them with the barrels of their weapons fixed at his chest. A silence drifted for some time.

"Mr Neals, hand over your weapon."

The silence began again, continuing for ten seconds before Albertine stepped out of the doorway.

"Inside, now. Everyone else, back on duty."

Harry followed her back into what had previously been the ballroom, now an office space with almost thirty young men and woman at computer stations. Harry followed Albertine up the staircase leading to her office, more guards lined the walls. Albertine sat behind her desk, there were no other chairs, intending to force Harry to stand. Harry approached the desk pushing her computer to the side, allowing himself to sit on the desk's edge. She shook her head, feeling displeased.

"I was summoned?"

"It seems you've made a full recovery. That's good, the tests seem to be going well."

Her tone was droll, expressing multiple shades of disappointment.

"The enemy have made contact. Their willing to deal."

"Why are you telling me this?"

"They won't talk to me unless you are present."

"This seems familiar, you couldn't get them to change their terms?"

"No, they were quite insistent, they handed over a few hundred civilians as a sign of good faith."

"Are they still chipped?"

"Yes, for the time being, if we try to operate, our enemy ensure us that they will kill them all."

"Where are they being kept?"

"A facility in the Jungle, we're isolating them for the time being."

"Where is the meeting taking place?"

"Broadland, we leave in an hour."

"An hour?"

"Is that a problem?"

She stood up from her desk, approaching the door way, Harry remained silent, still sitting on the desk. She turned around and faced him.

"Duncan passed away this morning."

She exited the room, Harry was left wondering, who, out of the two of them had cared less.

The man's shins were half shattered by the time he gave up the name. He was fourteen minutes to death before he gave up the location. Ray wiped the blood from the apron, placing it within a sink filled with ammonia. It was still early, the roosters were yet to crow; then again Ray had never heard or seen a rooster. He took a shower outside the barracks, starring up at the stars watching for trouble or change, it never came. Every day he would look up and visualise some projectile or another, blurring through the sky, just waiting to tear through his skull or burn him into powder. It didn't bother him much, in a way he revelled in it, contented by the probability that somewhere out in the wide world there was a bullet or a warhead with his name on it, and one day, while his mind was somewhere else, the source of his death would be fast approaching, and then he would be dead. He figured he was better off than most people, most people see their deaths coming, see the cancer, hear the murmurs, feel themselves slowly passing from the world. Bit by bit. Piece by piece. As the water struck him, he imagined the droplets as warheads, pummelling down upon him. The outdoor showers were one of the luxuries of the barracks, Ray enjoyed basking in the timid outdoor weather, making himself a better target for his would-be-assassins, always permanently lurking around the corners. Part of him wanted to die where he stood, wherever he stood, though the greater part of him did not wish to fall until his enemy fell first. He didn't want the parts of himself at odds with one another, so he tried not to look where he was going too carefully.

A young soldier strolled past, as Ray began to shut the water off. The young man caught a glimpse of Ray's naked, torn flesh, his hand quickly darted to cover his eyes. Ray stood there upright, quizzical, and naked.

"Private!"

The young man recognised Ray's voice immediately, snapping into a statue like salute. Ray let him stay there for some time, taking the occasional glances at the young man as he dried himself and got dressed.

"You're dismissed."

The young private darted back towards the direction that he had come from so fast that Ray couldn't help but feel offended. Was his body really that torn up? He traced the lines of scarring across his chest, the metal of his fingertips amply cool in the weather. All of his external augmentations were freezing, his skin remained its usual rubbery texture, he barely felt anything physical any more, too many dead nerves under too much scar tissue and dead skin. He spent the rest of the morning preparing various documents for various people and organisations. His office was a dark decrepit mess, piles of documents sitting on empty filing cabinets and storage places. Among the debris he felt most comfortable, he saw something in those small piles of powdered concrete. A large mass of crumpled pieces of papers began to form on his desk, every time he would find a document that he needed, he would crumple it up and throw it into a leather satchel, once the pile reached the brim he closed it, placed it on and continued down into the garage. With only two stairs to go he began to stumble and limp a little, he wondered if he had already broken something on his last expedition. He made a mental note to have it checked out. A few seconds later he forgot.

The driver held the door open for Ray, he threw the satchel inside before settling himself in and placing on his seat belt.

"You've got blood on your pants"

The driver attempted to inform him.

"Sorry, what?"

"You, have blood on your pants."

Ray looked at his thighs, sure enough a large stain had dried down his left pant leg.

"Thanks, for alerting me."

"Whose blood is that?"

"No clue."

"Right."

"Are you prepared for your meeting?"

"Not really, how did you know that I was heading for a meeting?"

"You're always headed for a meeting when you are on your way home."

"How did you come to notice that?"

"I've been driving you around for a while now."

He studied the driver's details. She was pretty and young, he believed her to be too young, still very much a teenager.

"Aren't you a little too young to be driving me?"

"You never felt that way before. I'm perfectly adept at driving."

"Before what?"

The silence continued for a number of seconds.

"Oh, before that, and it's not an issue of your driving ability, truly."

"Really? Then what exactly is the issue?"

"I have enemies in this world, I barely know any of their names, faces neither. This job will place you in the cross hair of these people."

"And that bothers you?"

"You are my driver, you are very dear to me!"

She let the moment sit for a few seconds.

"Is that true?"

"No. No it's not."

She continued along the road towards the city. Neither of them spoke a word for some time. Ray straightened out the pieces of paper as he prepared for his meeting.

"Who are the people you are meeting?"

"Is that really any of your business?"

"Well I'm almost certainly going to die in your service."

"Fair point. These people are enemies. They are wonderful, terrific people, but they will be my enemies."

"And why is that?"

"Because I want them to be."

"I don't follow. Why would anyone want enemies?"

Ray starred out the window, watching the trees pass by. He imagined figures crouched among the shrubbery, weapons in hand, ready to strike at any instant. He imagined the car bursting into a fiery wreck, his own body and that of the girl, torn to pieces, burned, unrecognisable.

"Some people are defined by their enemies, the forces they battle. I will be the force that they destroy. People forgive the occasional moral blunder when the enemy is a monster. They will be the victors and the world will forgive you all."

"Do they know this to be your plan?"

"They are far too honest and upright to suspect that I'm actually on their side."

"And I'm the only one who will ever know?"

"Yes, but you'll be dead soon enough."

The wharf was almost entirely vacant, Charles expected such since it was 4am. The lighthouse was the jewel of the harbour, Charles sat watching the small, moonlit waves crash against the wharf. The city behind him was larger and brighter than it had ever been before. He tried to pretend it didn't exist, he told himself that he would just sit on the bench and let himself grieve and if he survived, he would go off into the city, perhaps to the apartment described in the notebook. He sat and he wept, letting himself feel the confusion and pain. It came in a great flood, as each wave slammed against the wharf, he thought he was going to pass out, but he remained conscious. After two hours he stopped weeping. He had no more tears, just an ever-present, unrelenting state of nausea. He opened the note book.

'Ditch the car by the wharf.'

Charles retrieved the bag, before beginning his journey into the city. The sun began to rise behind him as he entered into a subway station. The station was relatively clean, Charles had no card for the train though he found that he didn't need one, a bright red sign read 'Free Transport.'

The trains ran every 10 minutes, Charles boarded, in a minute he had travelled the 8 kilometres to Southwark. Exiting out of the tunnel, the city was revealed. Step by step he continued into the city as it began to awaken. The cobbles below his feet were familiar, they looked like the ancient stones that he had known as a child only something was different. He soon came to the London Bridge, passing the hospital he had once worked at. He moved west, St Pauls visible in the distance. He began to jog, the bag heavy on his shoulder. He passed many of the churches and schools he had known form childhood, all of it was the same, plus or minus a few buildings. Charles felt as if he were stuck in some alternate universe where everything was just slightly off. Men and woman began to pour into the street, heading off to breakfast or work. Once Charles arrived at St Paul's Cathedral he entered inside, walking around the interior, it was all how he remembered it, only some unknown differences. The Cathedral had been destroyed in the war. He remembered holding pieces of the rubble in his hand, years before. Its apparent near perfect reconstruction perplexed him. Or perhaps he was remembering things wrong. A chart on the wall confirmed Charles's memory, showing all of the reconstructions of the church over the centuries, the version of St Paul's which Charles had known had been constructed in the late 17th century, after the great fire of London destroyed the previous St Paul's Cathedral. The reconstructed cathedral was destroyed in the war, having been rebuilt an only almost a year and a half before Charles awoke.

'The construction of the cathedral, like all of the recreations in London, was achieved through the use of building printers, reducing the cost and increasing the efficiency of construction significantly. This building, like all reconstructions belongs to the collective nation of England.'

Exiting onto the street, he looked through the communicator to find the address he was looking for. Returning once more into the subway he found his way through the intricate lines, taking a train from St Pauls to Marylebone, less than a minute passed and he was back on the street. He found his bearings and after a few minutes he arrived at a large Victorian building that had been split into four separate town houses. The second of the town houses was under his name though the instructions informed him to speak to the owner of the first of the town houses. It was almost 8am. Charles very much hoped that the owners were awake and home. Charles buzzed on the door, an all too familiar feeling of unease lingered in the pits of his stomach. A moment later a young man just departing the grips of puberty opened the door. His cheeks were overly round and he was wearing a maroon tie.

"Can I help you?"

The boy spoke with an accent that didn't quite collaborate with his decadent housing.

"Yes, I'm looking for the owner of this house, are they home?"

The boy looked suspicious, Charles realised the oddity of his sudden appearance, and he imagined that he didn't look too presentable either. The boy closed the door, calling his mother. After a moment Charles heard footsteps, the door opened once more to reveal the boy's mother; Claire.

Recognition occurred instantly, tears began to erupt from her eyes in a great rush. She cast open the door, grabbing him in her arms. A moment later, Charles found himself in the living room sipping tea. Claire continued to cry, though her eyes and mouth were smiling. Simon sat in the corner, clearly confused. The question was on both their minds, though Charles asked first.

"What happened?"

Claire took a minute, starring at the ceiling attempting to find the best answer to Charles's two word query.

"When you were imprisoned, a guard told me you had been killed. We stayed in Sector 23 for a few months, then moved to Sector 18. A few years later the civil war began. It turned out that *The Union* wasn't real, some malicious business men and women faked the whole thing, and *The Chairmen* was behind it all. The factories were exporting to the U.S, Indonesia and other countries. When that came out, some idealists from Europe countries took over, then they tried to turn London into a communist society, things fell apart fairly quickly."

She laughed a little as she realised the absurd words flowing from her memory.

"Before their leader was killed, someone contacted me, asking questions about you. I told them only a few minor details about your character. Tried to make you sound nice, non-threatening."

She paused for a moment.

"Then *The Chairman* dropped bombs on London, the communists dropped bombs on their side. Something happened to the communists and a man took over, he was another dictator, difficult and cruel. He made deals with hundreds of nations and societies. He disappeared and a group of intellectuals began to govern, real smart types. Around this time a young girl tracked me down. Taking me to this building, she gave us a large sum of money on the condition that I wait for you. I thought it were some type of screwed up game, but I thought I probably didn't have much of a choice. It's been about nine years and London's got much better. To be honest, I never thought I'd see you again"

Charles closed his eyes, pressing his head against the table. Sighing deeply.

"Where have I been all this time?"

Charles began to notice how much Claire had aged, before she had been 12 years younger than him, now Charles realised that she was now eight years older than himself.

"Just be glad that you're back I suppose. I'll show you to your place, then I'll have to get Simon off to work, I'll be back in two hours."

Charles nodded, following Claire outside to the neighbouring property. She unlocked it giving him the key card, they embraced once more before Charles entered. Claire walked away holding her son tightly by the arm. The house was three stories high, there were two bedrooms and two bathrooms. Charles placed his bag in the upstairs bedroom before continuing into the living room. The floors were made of polished concrete, the dining room table was positioned in the corner, a large bookcase lined the length of the wall, and a roller desk sat a metre from a substantial window looking out upon the busy street. Charles sat down at the desk, a worn copy of 'The Myth of Sisyphus,' by Albert Camus sat before him. A note attached to the cover.

'Dear Charles.

Life seems absurd and infinitely perplexing, or perhaps there is a plan, a God. I don't deserve a God, but you do. I'm sorry that all of this happened to you. I'm sure you'll want answers. You will not find any, none the less; it's not my position to tell you not to look.

I hope you find peace inside this wasteland.

Ray.'

Charles had no recollection of knowing a Ray, though the note made him feel both unnerved and comforted. He placed it within the back of the book as to preserve it. Grabbing some of the money in the bag, Charles left the building to explore his new surroundings, bumping into a woman as he exited his door. She dropped a small paper bag, Charles immediately crouched down to retrieve the bag and return it to its owner. She was roughly his age, her hair dark and long, she was wearing a red tweed jacket over a pair of brown trousers. She outstretched her hands to take the bag back. Charles only then noticed her metallic hands. She smiled and retrieved the package from Charles's frozen hands. Her lips were pink and perfectly symmetrical. Her smile was unwavering as she spoke.

"I think you may be my new neighbour."

Charles smiled and shrugged, the embarrassment rushing to his cheeks.

"I'm sorry. It's nice to meet you."

Charles held out his hand. The woman shook it before continuing down the street. She was a few metres ahead, when she turned her head and spoke.

"I hope that we will be fast friends, My Ryan."

She then kept walking. Leaving Charles to wonder how she had known his name. He watched her enter a café down the street. Charles followed her, sitting at a nearby table, he began to read.

'The Gods had condemned Sisyphus to ceaselessly rolling a rock to the top of a Mountain, whence the stone would fall back of its own weight. They had thought with some reason that there is no more dreadful punishment than futile and hopeless labor. If one believes Homer, Sisyphus was the wisest and most prudent of mortals. According to another tradition, however, he was disposed to practice the profession of highwayman.'

A beam of light, shown through the widow, igniting the strands of the woman's dark hair. She looked and caught him watching her. She smiled, but not like before, this was a mournful smile.

'I see no contradiction in this. Opinions differ as to the reasons why he became the futile laborer of the underworld. To begin with, he is accused of a certain levity in regard to the gods. He stole their secrets.'

The town was far smaller than Harry expected, it reminded him of the place that he did not grow up in. The buildings were all hundreds of years old, cramped together, moss and weeds rupturing through the ground, covering many of the buildings. Harry was the first off the helicopter. His shoes made a thud as they connected with the cobbles below. Albertine wasn't far behind, followed by a company of soldiers. Seconds later a helicopter arrived from the opposite direction, landing on the opposite side of the street. Five or more men dropped out of the helicopter. Approaching from the opposite direction, one figure entered into a small building towards the end of the street. Albertine and her company moved towards them, Harry not too far behind. The enemy's men stood in a line a few meters from the building. Albertine's men opposite them. Guns in the hands of each man, hovering half way pointed towards the ground.

Harry and Albertine entered the building passing closer to the enemy's men. Harry was first through the door, entering into a small room parted by a wooden rectangular table. At first Harry believed the room to be divided by a mirror set in the middle of the table. He saw his own face starring back at himself, only less raged, wearing different clothing, the oddity did not register for a moment, when it did, the shock rippled through him forcing the air out of his lungs. Albertine's response was much of the same. The figure smiled, it was clear that he had been expecting such a response.

"Please sit down."

Neither Harry, nor Albertine obliged. The man moved his hand into his jacket pocket, Harry drew his pistol aiming at the man's eyes, the same exact shade as his own.

"Easy, Harry, easy."

"How do you know my name?"

"Really? That's the question you ask? Well, I suppose I shouldn't be surprised."

"And why's that?"

Harry kept the gun trained on the man as he reached into his jacket, retrieving a communicator and placing it onto the table.

"Sit down, both of you."

Albertine took the first seat, Harry took the other a moment later. Albertine asked the next question.

"Who are you?"

"I'm the *Chairman.*"

"*The Chairman,* is dead."

"I know, I killed him."

"And now, you're the new *Chairman?*"

"Yes, but I never really wasn't, then again, '*The Chairman,*' as an entity doesn't truthfully exist."

The man looked lost in some trivial thought. Albertine slammed her hand against the table, Harry still had his gun trained.

"What the fuck are you talking about?"

"There is no need for such hostility, I was just saying that, '*The Chairman,*' is not a being but a construction, a persona that reflects power. You, and your terrorist friends in London may have destroyed this persona in London. In Liverpool, '*The Chairman,*' is alive and well."

"But you killed him."

Harry finally spoke again.

"Yes I did. He wanted that."

"You killed your father."

"He wasn't my father!"

The man lost his composure, letting out the words with hints of a scream. As his rage boiled over, lines appeared across his forehead, as if he suddenly aged a great many years, then returning back to relative youth as his composure returned.

"He was not my father, he told people he was, but he wasn't! I remember my father, he was scum. I remember growing up poor in my mother's kitchen. I remember both of them dying. They weren't my memories, they aren't yours either. He created me, in the pursuit of immortality, but I wasn't enough, just one version wasn't enough. He had to have the best version. So here we are. Me and you, engaged in a struggle that could last for an eternity."

"You did this to me?"

"I did this to myself. I created you out of nothing."

Albertine interjected.

"Charles Ryan, was nothing?"

The man needed no time to respond.

"History will remember him as such. He will be the shell out of which came my adversary."

"What do you want?"

Albertine began to rock in her chair, clearly enraged.

"To win, my way. Only you're not part of my plan."

She got to her feet.

"If you're threatening me, you should know that I recently acquired a number of predator drones, they are circling your city as we speak. Don't think I won't kill those people"

The man began to smile, Harry felt incredibly unsettled by the sight of his own menacing grin.

"How interesting. Well I suppose in the spirit of transparency, I should let you know that at least nine hundred citizens of Liverpool have fled the city, making their way to London. Would you like to see them?"

Then man tapped the display on his communicator, opening up a satellite view of London, hundreds of little red dots scattered throughout.

"So, where do we go from here?"

Albertine's face had drained of all its colour, her lips quivering.

"What do you want?"

"I want you to die, now. I want Harry to kill you. I want Harry to go back to London, raise an army, and do whatever it takes."

"Shoot him, Harry!"

Harry's hands were steady. His thoughts were a different matter. With no idea how to proceed he remained silent, the gun pointed at the man.

"Who was Jane Clements?"

The man's face stayed unmoved, no indication of surprise or guilt.

"She was a selfish bitch. She never loved Charles. She only did what was best for herself."

"You killed her!"

Albertine spat out the accusation. Harry knew he should have been enraged that the man had killed the innocent woman. He wasn't, he didn't care. Perhaps for the first time, Harry felt truly disgusted with himself. An implausibly confusing feeling. The man remained neutral.

"I did, and I don't regret it, her death was a necessity. You should be thanking me, Harry."

"I think you know, I'm not going to be doing that."

The man smiled once more.

"Have the urges begun yet? I'd imagine they would by now. Your previous employment kept you busy, but now, now you're just a baby sitter and an amateur surgeon."

Harry knew that he should have felt worried for Lucy, though his concern only reached as far as his own safety. The urges had begun, it wasn't quite bloodlust, but it was close. He wanted life in his hands, he wanted to let that life slip away. The previous day he had removed an inflamed appendix, from a seventeen year old male. He made the incision with ease, applying the clamps to the area. For a few moments he let his mind explore his dark desires, to leave the wound open, cutting a vein or artery, to watch the man regain consciousness as he bled out and faded from the world. Now at the table, Harry found himself ready to take a life.

"What's your name?"

The man continued to smile.

"You can call me M."

"Well, M, do you believe in God?"

As soon as the words were spoken the shot rang out. Harry didn't feel it tunnelling its way through his back, neither did he feel the round explode as it exited out his chest. He fell to the floor consumed by shock, bleeding profusely. A second shot rang out, colliding with Albertine's arm, she collapsed. Outside a fire fight took place. M sat at the table for a few more moments, walking to Harry, he dropped down onto his knee.

"I am God."

The next thing Harry saw was the face of a surgeon. The terrible pain registering for a moment, before he once again passed out. It would be two months until he awoke. A nurse in the room dropped his tablet the moment he saw Harry's eyes open. Rushing over to him. Grasping at his forearms. Harry didn't feel the nurse's grip entirely.

"Easy, easy."

He rubbed his hands together, he could feel the lines and contours, perhaps more sensitively then before, though something was unrecognisably different. The nurse tried to hold his arms down, even though the nurse was young and powerful, Harry still managed to break free. He starred at the back of his hand only to find shiny lines of metal. It looked as though his hands and arms has been encased in riveted silver.

"What did I lose?"

Harry whispered the words. The nurse moved closer unwrapping Harry's chest bandages to reveal an augmentation, the whole of the left side of his chest had been raised almost half an inch, covered in a material that looked like skin but felt closer to plastic.

A doctor walked into the room followed by the neurologist.

"How are you feeling Mr Neals?"

"I'm not Mr Neals."

The neurologist perked up, clearly intrigued.

"Charles?"

"No, but I do remember him, all of it."

"Who are you?"

"Call me, Ray Sancher."

"Why?"

"Because I don't want to be anyone else."

The prisoner gave up the location of the safe house and name of the soldiers running the operation. Ray arranged for the use of multiple helicopters and drones, in formation they flew towards Liverpool. The sky was almost entirely clear, as far as Ray knew all of the enemy's drones had been wiped out. Ray was almost giddy with excitement as the chopper approached the city. He looked to see the faces of the soldiers huddled around him, all of them stony and solemn, their lack of outward fear or excitement bored him. It would be the first time he made the trip without spending its duration gazing out at the sprawling forests below. He was too busy imagining his adventure to come. As soon as the helicopter touched down and the doors opened, he pushed his way to the front, making sure he was the first on the street, gun in hand racing off towards the facility. The soldiers sped off behind him, they were significantly fitter and faster than he was, since Ray's augmentations were slowly becoming less effective. A few civilians were sitting on the street smoking, Ray recognised one of them as a former cadet. They locked eyes for a moment before Ray again started running, he was a block from his destination when his drones arrived. Three drones sat 200 meters above the street, dropping three missiles each upon the building, Ray didn't wait for the dust to settle, before pulling down the goggles and rushing into the rubble. His enthusiasm betrayed him when he toppled over an iron rod that was jutting out of the ground. He was upright by the time the smoke cleared, a small circle of blood on his pant leg below his knee. The pain never arrived, it seemed that many of the nerves in his legs had begun to die since his augmentations had been damaged.

The smoke cleared to reveal a large metal door in the ground. A soldier placed a charge, a large explosion erupted. Not wasting a second, the soldiers tossed in multiple gas canisters, then fitting on their gas masks, they descended into the building. Ray wasn't the first, he regretted that, though he didn't wish to get in the trained soldiers way, he was consumed by vengeance but he didn't want anyone to die because of his bloodlust, well at least no one on his side.

Shots had been fired from both sides, Ray stepped over the body of one of his own men as the vastness of the room came into view. Few of the enemies had gas masks in reach when the smoke erupted, leaving them to choke on the concrete flooring, their limbs flailing. The room was divided by great aisles of weapons and supplies, Ray's soldiers divided and entered the aisles, each man's heart rate shown on each of the men's optical displays, if any man were hit, each soldier would be alerted. After ten seconds of venturing down the aisles a few enemy soldiers popped out of cover, they were put down in less than a second. The pilot of the helicopter set out a blast to each of the soldiers, there was only one signature left. Ray sprinted towards it, coming to the end of one of the aisles, behind a set of boxes came the sound of coughing and heavy breathing. Ray stepped around, pointing his rifle towards the source of the breathing. M sat toppled over on the floor, his hands clutching at a gaping bullet wound a few inches below his heart, the blood was pooling fast. Ray couldn't help but smile.

"We have a helicopter outside, we can get you to your lab, fix you up."

Ray giggled a little as he spoke. M did not feel look as delighted.

"I'm not telling you where it is."

"You'd rather die?'

M did not respond, avoiding Ray's gaze, Ray plunged a finger into his wound, M began to shriek with terror.

"I'll let you live, I'll let you go, I just want your machine."

"How can I trust you?"

Ray made an audible laugh. You know why. M gave a defeated smile.

"Even if you don't tell me, I bet I could keep you alive, at least for a while."

He placed his finger back into the wound. M screamed.

"O.K! I'll take you!"

The soldiers lifted M off his feet carrying him to the helicopter, Ray allocated the other helicopter and their men to retrieving whatever valuables lay inside the building. M was laid down inside Ray's helicopter, after M had given them the coordinates of his lab, he was placed on oxygen, Ray then applied bandages. The journey only took an hour, the coordinates leading them to an open field, Ray stepped out, forcing M to walk in front, they continued into a wooded area, arriving at a mass of overgrowth. M ripped at the greenery revealing a metal hatch. He pressed four numbers and the door slid open, they descended down a staircase into the facility, it was smaller than Ray had always imagined. He had always pictured a vast tower, rupturing from the sea, infinitely tall and impenetrably dark, hundreds of lab coats running around, beakers bubbling in the corner. In reality it was just a grey room with multiple monitors and strange pod sitting ominous in the middle of the room and an adjoined bathroom. M pressed a number of buttons on the monitor before undressing and collapsing into the pod, closing the door upon him, the machine went to work fixing his wound, Ray explored the monitors while the machine buzzed, he found an option called cryogenic-sleep, he waited for M's operation to be complete before selecting it. A loud humming noise began. Ray ascended back into the light, boarding the helicopter once more. When they were in the air a soldier approached him.

"What happened?"

"It was a dead end, he's dead."

The soldier dropped his gaze before returning to where he had been seated.

When they arrived back at the city, Ray had his driver take him home, inviting her in. Ray cooked a chicken and pasta dish with mushrooms. They sat down at table in the ballroom.

"How is it, that my fridge and pantry are always stocked? I barely ever sleep here."

"I do sometimes, most of this is my food."

"Anything else of yours here?"

"I keep my computer and clothes in a bag under the bed."

"Well you can move them into the dressers, soon enough."

"You found it?"

"Yes. I'll be leaving tonight, after a man drops off some things."

She looked down for a few moments.

"When will you be coming back? I mean, when will he be coming back?"

"I don't know, a few years. When things are better."

"What's going to you? What's going to happen to M?"

"I'm going to make it so that neither of us exist."

She placed her hands on her head, her elbows on the table. She began to weep.

"Why couldn't you have just stayed as Harry?"

"I never really stopped being Harry. That was the problem."

"You're not going to become M, you're different!"

"I think that's probably what M thought."

There was a large knock on the door, then the sound of a vehicle driving off into the distance. Ray mad no indication of movement, allowing himself to sit and watch Lucy. She was beautiful, he had always known so, always hated this knowledge. He was drawn to her, wanted her for himself. Only he knew what it would cost.

When Ray's gaze broke from Lucy, he found a small moth. Its wings were black and orange. At any other time, Ray would have thought it the most beautiful creature he had ever seen. In front of Lucy it was just a moth. It moved from his hand and began to dance with the light fixtures in the ceiling.

"Do you know what the main difference between most moths and a butterflies?"

He asked the question with his head arched, observing the dancing creature. Lucy's reply was quick and to the point.

"Night and day."

"Yes. Butterflies live their brief existences in the daylight. Moths live in the darkness, preyed upon by bats and spiders."

"So?"

She was beginning to become frustrated.

"So, what is the one thing a moth seeks more than anything else?"

She did not respond to his question.

"Light. I like to think that once an egg was laid on a leaf, more than one. This egg became a caterpillar, eating and shedding, eating and shedding. It lives in the day now and the night, it doesn't rest, and it just eats. Then it enters its cocoon and it tells itself 'I am going to be different. I'm not going to be like everyone else, I want sunshine, and I want sunshine. I want life, and I want sunshine,' then he emerges into the dark, but he keeps going. He finds a mate and they fly together, they mate in the sunshine. And maybe the eggs know, maybe they wake up in the sunshine, maybe they create a new species. An egg, a caterpillar, a moth, an egg, a caterpillar, a butterfly, an egg. What's next? "

Lucy's face formed the shape of confused sadness.

"You're not a moth, you're a person!"

"I'm not so certain."

Ray traced the lines of his collar bone, traced where it stopped being bone and turned into metal. Ray got to his feet as he spoke.

"We'll talk again soon."

"When?"

"When things are safer. I'll need you to make arrangements for Charles."

Ray produced a communicator from his pocket, sliding it across the table.

"All of my money is yours, when the others take over. Give them the information they want, but only what they want."

She nodded. He walked upstairs and filling one bag with clothing and another filled with a collection books, several hundred, he would get through them all in only a couple of years, he stored hundreds more on a tablet. Returning to the dining room that had once been an office and previously a ballroom. He walked to the door. She followed him out into the night air.

"You were the best friend I ever had."

Ray smiled looking to the ground.

"Same, that's why I can't keep you in danger."

"I love you, Harry."

"I love you too, Lucy."

Ray got in the car. Almost the entirety of which was filled with the bags, as well as containers of rations and equipment. He drove off into the night.

He set up a camp bed in the middle of the bunker, packing a collection of medications into a cabinet in the bathroom. He lay down.

It would take him a year to learn how to operate the machine, another year to code the stem cells to Charles's DNA. Spending the following years waiting for Lucy's call. He wrote stories in his head, pondering the details of identity, personality and existence, it seemed to him that there were no conclusions to be found. None that he could find at least.

Eventually the communicator rang. Ray answered it almost immediately, he always kept it close by.

"Hello."

There was a long silence.

"It's time."

There was another long silence.

"Would you please, send me a copy of the information that Charles will need. Also did my 'enemies' take control?"

"What's going to happen to you?"

"Answer my question."

"Yes, they took over. We're part of the European Union now. Now tell me, what's going to happen to you."

"I'm going to kill M."

"There is no M!"

"There never will be, not anymore."

"I don't understand."

Lucy began to cry.

"Please send the documents."

Ray could only hear her tears and nothing else. A second later he felt the communicator buzz in his hand, he briefly searched through the documents.

"Thank you."

Silence.

"I hope you are happy, Lucy. I really hope you made something of yourself."

"I did."

"That's wonderful. Goodbye, Lucy."

She was again silent.

"Is this really what you want?"

"It is."

She hung up. Ray spent the next few hours copying out the details into a blank leather notebook, he enjoyed the feel of the task immensely, and he wondered whether the man in the pod would feel the same. He wrote the letter next, coming to its close he felt a strange sense of serenity, it washed over him in a wave of contentedness washed over him. He placed 1.2 million Euros into the bag, followed by the notebook and letter, dropping the communicator in last. Ray walked up the stairs to the door, opened it revealed a night sky filled with thousands of stars. He walked to the car, weeds and moss had overrun the exterior of the vehicle, he opened the door, pressing the ignition, it came to life. He descended downstairs, retrieving the body from the pod. Dragging it up stairs and placing it into the back seat, he was heavier than Ray had expected, the augmentations his arms losing functionality. Once the body was in the car, Ray entered the wrong code on the lock, his actions quickly followed by a barely audible explosion. He laughed to himself, the wring code thing had been a guess, the accuracy of which confirmed in his head what he was doing. Ray drove off into the distance, he had intended to go as far as the city, though he was unsure of what had changed since he had last been, though he trusted his enemies, knew that the world they formed would be a good one. He settled on an abandoned and dilapidated factory several hours drive from the city. Carrying the bag and the body inside. Ray cleaned the car as best he could.

The sun began to rise, it was the first time he had seen natural light since he left the city. He spent the entirety of the morning just staring into the blue of the sky. He found it to be both beautiful and terrifying. The air was cleaner now, the landscape less scared.

Around midday, Ray heard the screams coming from inside the building, drawing the pistol with a shaking hand, he walked into the darkness for the last time.

www.ingramcontent.com/pod-product-compliance
Lightning Source LLC
Chambersburg PA
CBHW071217260626
47162CB00004B/1318